THE LORDLY ONES

By the same author

THE FURIES

THE INNER WHEEL

PAVANE

MACHINES AND MEN

THE BOAT OF FATE

ANITA

THE CHALK GIANTS

THE GRAIN KINGS

LADIES FROM HELL

MOLLY ZERO

KITEWORLD

KAETI AND COMPANY

THE LORDLY ONES

by

KEITH ROBERTS

Wildside Press
Berkeley Heights • New Jersey

Wildside Press
PO Box 45
Gillette, NJ 07933-0045
www.wildsidepress.com

CONTENTS

The Lordly Ones 7

Ariadne Potts 29

Sphairistike 53

The Checkout 80

The Comfort Station 101

The Castle on the Hoop 116

Diva 131

THE LORDLY ONES

'How beautiful they are, the Lordly Ones,
'Who live in the heart of the hollow hills.'
—*William Sharp, Rutland Boughton, 'The Immortal Hour'*

When I was very young I was given a pedal car. That must have been just before the War, as such things later became unobtainable. I mean by that World War Two. People of my generation still call it 'The War', though of course there have been many wars since.

It was a very fine car indeed, much larger than was common and with a door on one side that could be opened. It was painted a bright golden brown, with three smart red flashes on either side of its bonnet. It had streamlined headlamps let into its mudguards and its wheels had rubber tyres and chromium hub plates, though the hub plates could not be removed. I became very skilled at driving it, though perhaps I should not say such a thing, and could negotiate the narrowest gates and doorways without scraping its paint. I also learned to steer it in reverse, and was able to turn it round in very small spaces.

I do not know why my father gave me such an expensive present as we were a fairly poor family. I was an only child, and lived in an end terrace house in a back street of the town in which I had been born. Both the terrace and the street in which it stood have been knocked down now for many years.

It was a small house, though as a child I was not conscious of this, but it had a long garden. I remember the garden particularly well. It was closed off on both its sides, partly by solid fencing and partly by trellis work fixed to stout posts. The fences and trellis were painted with creosote, which the summer sun bleached to a pleasant brown. At the bottom of the garden was a tall, untidy hedge of hawthorn. The hedge had gaps in it low down through which you could see allotments dotted with little sheds, and pig pens made of corrugated iron. On a sunny day the allotments and the men working on them looked like little bright pictures seen through the stems and leaves.

The garden, though narrow, was further divided by two long paths made of some pinky ashy stuff and edged by a grey-leaved creeper that grew star-shaped flowers in summer. Near the house was a little paved part my mother always called The Patio. Beyond The Patio was a rose plot, then another with Lane's Prince Albert apple trees, then the vegetable patch and some raspberry canes before you came to the cold frame and the compost heap. There was a little greenhouse too, built close up to the hedge so that one side of it always grew green spots on the glass no matter how often they were scraped away. The greenhouse had an iron rainwater butt. During the War my father put it outside in the street and wrote FIRE on it in big red letters, though we were never bombed.

I remember the garden so well because of a game I played there. All the paths had names I had invented, the long paths and the little ones that went between the plots, the hard, beaten patch by the compost heap, the turning place beside the cold frame. The borders had their roadways too, places that were not often dug and where my tyre marks did not show, but only I knew what they were called. On summer afternoons when I did not have to shop with my mother I would sit on The Patio and plan my travels through the country I had invented. My choice of routes was wide. For instance, I could take the North Road or the South. The North Road, the first of the long pink paths, led to Foxglove Close, or if I travelled its full length, to Cold Frame Garage and the greenhouse. Behind the greenhouse were old bricks and rotted boxes, and a pair of great spoked wheels my father told me had once belonged to an aeroplane. The bindweed crawled over them before climbing up into the hedge. The Road ended here. It was a dangerous place, frightening and a little dark. Or I could cross The Patio to the South Highway. Clumps of violets grew between the flags of The Patio, where the cracks were widest. I knew exactly the locks to apply to steer my wheels between them. From the Highway I could swing right into Mornington Crescent. The grass path in front of the raspberry canes curved a little, and it was here the sun came first in summer. I do not know where I had heard the name I chose for it, but it seemed right.

Wherever I travelled though, I would always end up in my favourite place of all. I called it Daisy Lane, from the big mauve clumps of Michaelmas Daisies that grew close by each year. Here, by careful reversing, I could slide myself right out of sight between tall bushes. Once in position I could not be seen from the house at all, but *I* could see. I could stare down through the gaps in the hedge at the men working in the field, easing the car backward a little by the pressure of a pedal if one of them paused and seemed to glance my way. The sun struck hot on my face and arms, and the bushes broke the breeze. It was always still in Daisy Lane, and wasps would come and bite at the old wood of the fence posts, little beetles would run across the earth.

In winter or when the weather was bad I would oil the motor ready for fresh journeys, and polish its headlamp rims. Newspapers would be spread on the living room rug and my father would turn the car on its side for me so I could reach the pedal bearings. I had been given a little oilcan, round, flat and with a long, thin spout, to have for my own. I kept it with my cleaning rags in a tin with an overlapping pattern in brown, gold and orange. The oilcan had to be stored upright, or the oil would spill.

I do not know why I have begun to write down my thoughts, or why I should think first of my toy car, and the games I played when I was small.

It is very still today, with hardly any wind, and the Station is quiet. Recently a skylight ventilator has taken to rattling, several times it has woken me in the night. Yesterday I got the big steps out and climbed up to it but I could not see what was wrong. I wonder if a strip of draught excluder would be a good idea. If I put it along the top of the frame by the catch it would stop the noise, and also prevent the rain getting in. At least it would do no harm. I am always careful about undertaking actual repairs, as I know I am not very good with my hands.

I did my first piece of writing last night. I have read through it, and do not quite know what to think. I am not really sure what I am trying to do. I am certainly not writing my life story.

Even if I was capable of such a thing, it would not be of any interest. Nor am I keeping a diary, I did the writing in an old ledger I found when I first cleaned my office out. So I suppose I must have started a hobby. I must be careful not to let it interfere with my work. I do not think I have ever had a hobby before.

The writing took a long while. Three hours, from locking the Stations until nearly midnight. I was amazed when I looked at my clock and saw how much time had passed. If I am to write regularly I must rearrange my schedule so as to take more advantage of the light. I have a good supply of candles but it seems a waste to burn them unnecessarily.

I read parts of what I had done several times. I was surprised at how much I had remembered about being small. I could never be a real writer of course but I find I can put my thoughts down clearly, and in the proper order. That will have to do instead.

I must spend this afternoon filling the water tank. It is a good tank and has been very useful, but filling it takes a long time. I found it behind what I think is an old factory on the far side of the Car Park. It was thrown out on a rubbish heap with a lot of used bricks so it seemed quite all right to take it, though it was very hard work getting it to the Station. I was afraid to drag it in case I damaged it but it was so heavy that carrying it took most of a day. It had a tap already fitted that I thought would be very useful, though when I got it back I realized it would have to be lifted up onto something before I could fill buckets from it. So I fetched some of the bricks and made them into two stacks for it to stand on. I was very pleased when I had finished as it seemed to be quite firm. The night after I fixed the tank was the first time I saw the camp fires on the hills.

A stream runs past the Station, within a yard or two of it, but the banks are steep and slippery and it is difficult to reach the water. For a time I did not know what to do, then I found something in a shed by the rubbish heap that I thought would help. It was like a little crane with a pulley and an arm and a sort of foot, a metal plate with holes at the corners for fixing. I do not know what it was for originally. There was some rope too. At first I did not like to borrow it as I was afraid it would look like stealing, but there was nobody I could ask.

There is a bridge across the stream, where the cars used to

come into the Car Park. I managed to fix the crane to its parapet with baling wire. The pulley was very stiff at first but it ran quite freely after I had oiled it. It was difficult for a time getting the bucket to fill. Instead of turning over and sinking it would float, and the current would carry it off along the stream. I found after several tries that it was best to drop it the last little way with a bump, and sort of jog it over onto its side. Of course I only have the plastic buckets that were supplied for use on the Station. I wonder if metal ones might work better.

I was very worried when the water went off. I did not bother so much about the electricity as I had a box of candles in the office and have been able to get more since, but without water the Stations could not do their job properly. There was water in the small cisterns of course, but the big one my side used to flush automatically every twenty minutes and without the sound of it the whole place seemed different. I got the steps and filled it with a bucket. I found it would still work when the water reached the proper level. At first I filled it several times a day but with nobody using the Station any more that was not really necessary. But it is still done twice a day, last thing before I lock up and first thing in the morning.

I have been thinking some more about when I was small. I have been trying to remember the very last time I used the car, drove down the South Highway or into Mornington Crescent. There must have *been* a last time, but I cannot remember it. This seems strange. I found the car a long while later, when I was cleaning out the wash house after my mother died. It was very rusty, it needed a good clean up and a coat of paint. There were new people next door, with young children. I asked them if they wanted it but they said no so I put it back where it was. It was hard to believe I had once been small enough to drive it. By that time most of my Roads had gone anyway, as my mother had been ill for several years and I was never very good at gardening. It disappointed my father, as he had wanted me to be a gardener like himself.

I did not get on very well at school. Everybody said I was slow, though I was never sure just what they meant. One time when it was very bad I started trying to do all sorts of things, like eating and tying my shoelaces, quicker than usual to show I was not slow at all. My father visited the school several times. I met him once in the corridor, it seemed very strange to see him there. Afterwards the Head sent for me, from one of my classes. I was very frightened. He asked me a lot of questions about the sort of things I did at home. I could not answer him properly as I did not know what he meant. It was a new school, built nearly outside the town, and his study was very new with light green walls. There was a cream-painted cupboard behind his desk, I knew that was where he kept his Sticks. They were canes really but we called it getting the Stick. There were also tall glass doors with a flagged courtyard outside, like The Patio at home only much tidier. He said he wanted to help me and that I was not to worry. I was very glad when he told me I could go.

After that they put me into a Special Class. They said it was to help my reading. We all sat round on funny-smelling straw mats with bright patterns on them and took it in turns to read aloud. I could read quite well although I was never very interested in books, but I could not answer questions. They confused me, I could never understand what I was supposed to say.

Afterwards the Head sent for me several more times and asked what I was doing at home to help my mother. I could never think of what to say to him either. He said he wanted to be my friend but I never really liked him much.

I think not being able to remember the last time I drove my car is really odd. It has made me think of doing other things for the last time. I did read a story once, about a man who was going to be shot for spying. Only they did not do it till the morning so that he could see his last sunset. But if you were going to be killed there would be a lot of other things. Like the last time you cut your nails, or the very last time you ever combed your hair.

Things always seemed to get harder for me, not easier. After I left school my father got me a job at the Council nurseries. I had to go and see a man called Mr Sanderson. I thought I was going to like it at the beginning. It was not far to go, just the other side of the allotments. There were three big greenhouses about 30 yards long. I could see the roof of our house and the big hedge at the bottom of the garden, it looked quite different from the other side. But I did not do very well. I kept breaking plant pots, things were always going wrong. And there was a girl who worked in the office. She used to follow me about, try and get me on my own in one of the sheds. She made me afraid to go to work. Then she said a lot of things about what I had done to her. They were not true but everybody believed her. Afterwards I worked at the Tip for a long time, then I was on the carts. I did not like that at all.

I was nearly 45 when I started at the Station. It had not been built very long then. I knew they wanted someone to look after it but I did not think they would give the job to me. I had to see a man called Mr Ireland. That was at the new Council Offices. He asked me a lot of questions, it was nearly like being in the Headmaster's study again. Then he said that I had worked for the Council a long time and that apart from one small incident I had a very good record. He said that he had known my father for many years and that he had been a good worker too. He made some notes and sat and thought for a minute, then he said he would let me know. He was very nice to me.

The letter came next day. It upset my mother very much. I was really happy, I could not understand why she was not pleased as well. She kept saying, 'To think a son of mine should be a lavatory attendant.' But I never thought of it as a lavatory. It was the Station almost from the start. I heard a lady say one afternoon, 'Thank God, a Comfort Station!' It pleased me very much, it seemed such a good name. I think she was an American.

There are two Stations really, built on to each other, one for Ladies and one for Gentlemen. The Ladies side was looked after by someone called Mrs Stevens. She was rather short and had hornrimmed glasses and very yellow hair. On sunny afternoons she used to take a chair outside and sit by her door and knit. I used to say good morning to her but we never talked much. She did not seem very friendly.

I expect it will sound silly but I think the Station is very beautiful. It stands to one side of the Car Park, very close to the stream. It is low and plain and built of a sort of fawn-coloured brick, with narrow windows along the side that have muffled glass. Inside, all the tiles are white and the walls are a very light grey with more white on them in little splashes. It is always cool, even in summer. At the end farthest from the stream there is quite a large room with one door into the Station and another that opens outside. This is my room. It has a chair and table and a ring for boiling kettles, a sink and two big cupboards and quite a lot of shelves. There is even space for a bed, which is very fortunate.

I made a mistake about the room the first time Mr Ireland came to the Station. I had been there nearly 2 weeks then. When I took over it was in a terrible mess, with cigarette ends ground out all over the floor and dirt everywhere. I scrubbed it out, using the disinfectant for the Station floor, and got everything tidy, and Mr Ireland came to see what stores and equipment I had and what new things I would need. I said, 'If you will come into the office, sir, I will show you,' and he laughed. I felt myself going red at that, like I used to at school when I had said something stupid, but he put his hand on my shoulder. 'That's all right,' he said. 'If you want it to be your office, that is what it will be.' I do not know why, but I felt better almost at once.

The next time he came it was because I had written him a note. One of the channels was stained, it annoyed me as the rest of the Station was spotless, but although I had scrubbed it with the disinfectant for a long time it had not done any good. Also people kept writing things on the cubicle doors. Horrible things, sometimes. I had been rubbing them off with hot water and Vim but the paint was wearing away as well in places and the doors were looking a sight. He brought me a can of special cleaner that worked very well though he told me to be careful not to get it on my hands. He said he would get some special paint put on the doors. He even asked me what colour I would like. I said I thought dark blue would look very nice and he laughed. He said it was up to the architect really but he would see what he could do. I felt confused. Nobody had ever asked me a thing like that before.

I asked him if he would like a cup of tea. I do not know what made me say such a thing as it was hardly my place. I was sure he would refuse and that I had made another mistake but he said, 'That would be very nice.' I was a bit nervous, I gave him the cup with the big crack in it, I did not realize till afterwards. But he did not seem to mind. He sat in the office and smoked a cigarette. Then he said a most surprising thing. 'You know,

Tom,' he said—he always called me Tom, right from the start—
'if everybody on the Council was as conscientious as you, we'd
have no call for complaint.' I did not know what to say. I felt
really embarrassed, being praised like that. I had never realized
there was anything I could do well.

After that I started coming down to the Station very early. It
opened at half past eight in the summer and I was suppose to be
there an hour before, but I took to coming down at half past six.
It gave me a chance to do a lot of extra cleaning jobs, like the
door catches and the windows. It was a lovely time of day, with
nobody about and the sun on all the buildings and the parked
cars. There was mist on the stream sometimes, but the hills all
round the town were very clear.

Sometimes I would stay on late as well, after the Station was
closed. Then I would not want to go home at all. My mother had
died by this time and they had moved me out of the old house.
They gave me a flat in a new building overlooking the Cathedral
Close. It was very nice, there was a bedroom and a place where I
could cook, but I did not like it. I was always happier at the
Station.

I thought about it a long time, then I bought a little air bed.
They had a sale of camping things at one of the big shops in the
town centre, that was what gave me the idea. After that I could
sleep at the Station and get up and make my breakfast and start
whenever I liked. Each morning I rolled the bed up carefully
and put it away at the bottom of one of the cupboards. I did not
tell Mr Ireland. I did not think he would approve.

After he brought the cleaning stuff he started calling in quite
regularly, sometimes twice a week. He always had tea. He would
sit and talk about his job, and how hard it was to keep everything
going with the money getting tighter all the time. One day he
even brought some tea of his own, he said it was to replace all
mine that he had drunk though that did not matter. It was a very
expensive brand, one I had never bought. I still have some of it
left.

I do not know how to describe Mr Ireland. He was about 2
inches taller than I am, with grey hair combed straight back and
very bright blue eyes, but that is not enough. There were other

things, and I cannot find the proper words for them. Nobody was ever as kind to me as he was.

I have been trying to remember how long it has been since anybody used the Station. The Trouble came at Easter, and it is nearly autumn now. So it must be at least 5 months, perhaps more.

I have fixed the skylight, though I do not know yet whether it has worked as it has not been windy. Also, I looked out of the office window tonight before I lit the candle. There seemed to be a lot more fires than before, and some of them were closer.

I must stop now, as the candle is nearly out. I did not mean to go on for so long, but there was more to say about Mr Ireland than I realized.

I want to try and write something very difficult. I have started twice already and had to cross out what I had done. I think perhaps this is the first really hard thing I have tried to say.

There was a song we had to learn at school, about the Lordly Ones. Miss Chaston, who taught us music, said that meant the fairies. It was a strange song and puzzled me very much at first. It said they lived in the hollow hills but I thought the other children were singing 'the Harlow hills' and that all fairies lived at a place called Harlow, wherever that might be. I often used to make mistakes like that.

I did not think about the song again for years. Then when I was working on the dust carts there was a man called Smudger. I never knew his proper name. He was a big man, much bigger than me, and had a lot of friends. I used to go with him sometimes to a hotel near the town centre to have a drink. I would never have dared go to such a place on my own. The Public Bar was up the yard and to get to it you had to pass a room lit by candles where all the guests were eating their dinner. The first time I looked in I thought some of the ladies were the most beautiful I had ever seen and for some reason I remembered the song at once. I knew they were not fairies of course, just very rich people, but afterwards whenever I went there the song always started in my mind.

Then when I had my flat I used to sit quite a lot looking down over the Cathedral wall at the grass and driveways inside, especially if there was a wedding there or some other big function, which often happened. The people who came were very grand. Some of them even wore top hats like in the films, so I thought they must be the Lordly Ones too. So although I was always getting shouted at for being clumsy or in the way, I thought if I could get the job at the Station some of them might come there and see the towels all clean and soap in the dispensers, and be pleased. I wonder if Mr Ireland knew that, and that was why he set me on.

I have had an idea. There is some old lead piping on the rubbish heap where I found the water tank. If I could somehow fix a piece of it to the edge of one of the buckets it would tip over automatically when it went into the water, and filling it would be a lot easier.

I cannot do very much tonight. I feel tired. I wonder if it is the writing, and having to think so hard to find the proper words.

It works! I went over to the factory first thing this morning, as soon as it was light, and brought the pipe back. I cut a piece off, using a saw that was in one of the cupboards in the office, and knocked it flat with a hammer. Then I bent it round the edge of one of the buckets and hammered it again till it was tight. After that I did not have to jiggle the bucket about each time to make it sink, and filling the tank took a whole half hour less!

After I had finished I went and sat on the bank of the stream for a time because I was still feeling shaky from having had to use the saw. I do not like saws. I was playing with one once when I was small and it slipped, I remember looking down and seeing all the white bone. I could not feel anything at first so I thought I had not hurt myself very much, then the blood all came in a big red spurt. I think everybody in the street came out to see when I was taken to the hospital. My mother kept shouting, 'I told him not to touch the saw! I told him not to touch the saw!' I do not think I was so frightened of the blood as of being shouted at again if the saw had slipped. It made me feel really sick. But it had not slipped, I had not had an accident at all, and after a time the sickness went away.

It is a very beautiful stream. There are notices on the bridge saying it is the River Avon so I suppose it must be, but it always looks like a stream to me. Under the bridge the water is quite deep but by the Station there is a shallower part where there are great masses of starwort. The underwater leaves are long and thin like hair but those on top spread out like little light green roses. There is duckweed too. In the very shallowest parts the leaves throw their shadows onto the bottom, each with a little bright rim. Hart's Tongue Ferns grow on the banks. Their leaves are bright green and wavy, and the tips of the longest nearly touch the water. There are small trees too, mostly alder. When I first went to the Station I bought a book of plants, and can now identify nearly all of them.

I was always afraid they would do something to the stream, dredge it or culvert it. I remember when they cut the hedge behind the old house. It was only waist high when they had finished, all the branches woven in and out like a fence, and the dark places underneath it had gone. Everything looked different, it did not seem possible there had ever been that great mound of leaves.

I used to sit by the stream a lot, early in the morning and in the evening when the Station had closed. I was there when the Trouble started. It was a fine evening. It was a Sunday, so there were not many cars in the Park. I did not understand what was happening at first. There was some shouting, and bangs and rattlings like a lot of cars all backfiring at once. I only realized later it was shooting.

By that time I was sleeping at the Station nearly every night. I had bought a little gas cooker as I was afraid to use too much electricity, and I had a saucepan and some tins of soup. When I heard the shooting I was very frightened. I could not think what to do. In the end I decided to stay in the office and wait. I locked the doors and went to bed. Some people came in the night and took the rest of the cars away, but they did not come near the Station.

The noise went on all next day, and most of the next. The third morning was very quiet, and there was no electricity.

Two days later the water stopped running. I knew I must do something then, as it had to be reported. Also I was very hungry, having used up all my soup. There was a telephone box in the main street, at the top of the little lane that leads to the Car Park. I made sure I had some twopenny pieces and walked up to it. My throat felt rather dry as I do not like using telephones.

The main street was empty. There were some cars parked, one with its doors standing open, but nobody was moving about. Also there was a big cloud of smoke coming from somewhere behind the Cathedral. It was all very odd.

I rang the Offices. I had the number in my pocket book. I was going to ask to speak to Mr Ireland but the telephone did not answer. It did not even make those little clicks and buzzes you usually hear. I read the instructions to make sure I was doing it right, and tried again. But nobody spoke.

After I had tried several more times I went back to the office. It was a sunny morning, quite warm for the time of the year. I made some tea. I had to drink it without anything as I had run out of both sugar and milk. I did not know what to do, I had been relying on speaking to Mr Ireland.

It was afternoon by the time I had decided. I walked round to the Offices. The doors were all closed. I banged on them but nobody came. I felt more confused than ever and went on toward the town centre. I had not gone very far when I saw a body. I mean a dead person. He was lying on the path with his arms spread out and there were dark brown splashes all round his head. I had not seen anything like that before.

I kept on walking but I soon saw some more. One was a lady. She had some shopping with her, it had all spilled out across the path. Something, cats I expect or perhaps birds, had been scratching at it so that all the cartons were spoiled. I did not go very close.

There were a lot more bodies in the town centre and more cars, one with its windscreen smashed. The bodies were mostly on the pavements, so I walked in the road. I kept looking round. I was expecting somebody to shout at me to ask what I was doing. It took me a long time to realize that there was nobody left.

On the way back I passed the supermarket where I used to do my shopping. Its doors were standing open and one of its windows had been broken. I went inside. I was not hungry any more after what I had seen but I knew I had to get more food. I took a basket and went round some of the shelves. They were all still full. I took some corned beef and some tins of fruit salad, which I have always liked. I knew it was no use taking the bread as it would have gone stale but I found some things called oat cakes that were just as good. When I had filled the basket I went back to one of the checkouts. I did not know how much I had taken and am not very good with figures, so I left a 5 pound note in the clip on the front of the till. I hoped that would be enough.

I went back again when the food was gone. It was horrible. There were big crows flapping about in the streets and the whole town was starting to smell. I knew I had to have a lot of food this time as it might be a long while before anyone came back, so I took a shopping trolley. I tried to add it all up but I kept getting different amounts. In the end I just walked away. I knew that was stealing but I was very hungry, and somehow it did not seem to matter any more.

I do not know why the Trouble happened. There was a lot on the telly about the black people fighting the whites, and the Unions trying to take over, but I could never understand it. I do not know why black people and white people should fight. I knew a black man once when I was on the carts. He was a very quiet person, and used to bring small fruit pies to work that his wife had made. He shared them with me sometimes. They were very nice.

I have done more than I intended to again, the ledger is starting to look quite full. But it seems when I think of one thing it makes me think of others, and then they have to be put down as well.

I am glad I have written about what it was like in the town. I do not feel quite so worried now, though I do not know why that should be.

I had a bad dream last night. It was very frightening. At least I think it was a dream. It certainly started out as one.

When it began I was sitting by the back door of the old house in my car. I remember it very clearly. There was a patch of dark blue shiny bricks and a strip of earth to one side with ferns in it and a big flaky seashell the size of a football. The outhouse door was painted dull green and had a horseshoe nailed to it. I never liked to get too close to the outhouse as there was something inside it that frightened me. I found out later it was an old washing dolly but in the half light it always looked like an animal, with a long neck and big sticking-out ears. In the dream I knew it was going to come out and get me but I could not move. My mother was knocking on the living room window and shouting something, but it was as if the pedals of the car were frozen solid.

Then I do not know how it happened but I had moved and was rushing across The Patio very fast. Only the garden was not as I remembered it, there was a great hill beyond that kept getting steeper and steeper. The pedals started going quicker and quicker, then just as I was going to crash there was a great shout of 'Whoa, back!' It woke me and I sat up. I was sweating quite a lot. I was frightened because the shout had been right too. I mean, something I remembered. The house I used to live in was on a little slope and there was one Co-Op man who never used to set the handbrake on his van, and that was how he would shout at the horse when it kept walking on. The noise still seemed to be echoing, though why he should come back and shout in my office again after so long I could not understand.

I lit a candle, but there was nothing there. Then I thought the sound might have come from one of the Stations, my side or the Ladies, so I got the keys and a torch and unlocked them. But everything was all right. It was a beautiful night with a full moon. The hills showed clearly, and I could hear the stream running in the dark.

I did not go into the other Station till nearly a month after the Trouble. Mrs Stevens did not come again, though with all that had happened I hardly expected her to, so while my side was still opened and closed at the proper times hers stayed shut. Then one morning, I do not know why, I tried my outside key in the other lock. I did not think it would fit. But it did, and the door opened.

I was very startled by that. For a moment I did not know what to do. Then I put my head inside. Naturally I had never been in before. It was just like my side, the same light grey walls, the same basins and roller towels and white tiles. It smelled a little musty though, from having been shut up so long.

I went farther in. I was worried that I was doing wrong, but very curious. There were no channels, naturally, just the cubicles, but everything else was just the same, with a door at the back to another little office. It was open, so I went in. It was the same as mine, only not so tidy. There was a raincoat on a hanger and a corner cupboard and a table with some keys on it. I took them and put them on my own ring. I was not worried any more as I had come to a decision. Since nobody was looking after the other Station it was clearly my duty to take it over myself. This time I was sure Mr Ireland would agree. I went back and stood in the main part again by the cubicles. It still seemed a little strange, everything the same as my side only the wrong way round. But I soon got used to it.

My first job was to clean out the office, which was really in rather a mess. I tidied all the stores I could find and washed the floor, and stood the doors open for it to dry. Then I started on the rest. I cleaned the pedestals, flushed all the cisterns and refilled them by hand. There was a dispenser on the wall that I did not like to touch at first but finally I unlocked it. I did not know what I would see inside but it was quite all right, just a stack of little white cartons. I had found some while I was tidying the office and had not known what they were. I filled the machine right up and checked that it was working properly, then I started on the floor. A lot of dust and stuff had blown in under the door, I swept it out and gave the Station a good scrub through. Then I got the steps and cleaned the windows, inside and out. It was a hard day's work but when it was finished I was very pleased with myself.

Next morning I went back to the town. I had realized while I was doing the cleaning that the other office would make a useful store room, and since my food was running low I had better get a really good supply. The streets did not smell quite as much as they had, though in the supermarket it was worse. All the food in the refrigerators had gone bad and there were rats scuttling about. They had even chewed the labels on a lot of the tins so it seemed I was only just in time. I spent a long while going forward and back with the trolley. When I had finished the office was really full. Then I went looking for other things that would be useful, like spare gas cylinders for the cooker. It was easy, as nearly all the shops had been left open. I had got quite used to taking what I wanted by this time, it hardly seemed like stealing any more. After all nobody else wanted it. Then I went to my flat. I had some more tinned soup there, I took it all and some clothes and blankets.

Nearly the last thing I did was go to the Cathedral. I had wanted to see inside it ever since I could remember but I had never dared, and now seemed as good a chance as any. When I got up close I realized how big it really was, with the spire going up and up in the sunlight and all the windows staring down. It made me feel quite giddy. I half expected it to be locked up but it was open too. There was a big door at the side, standing ajar. I went through and there was another door with a huge iron handle. I turned it and pushed and it opened a little way. The air inside smelled funny, very musty and cold. There were great tall columns like trees and a big window with the light all pouring through. But I could not go in. I stood on the step a long time but in the end I had to walk away. It frightened me. Places like that are for the Lordly Ones, not the likes of me.

I spent this afternoon sitting by the stream again. The doors of both Stations were open, ready for anybody who might come, and there was nothing else to do. It was a warm afternoon and very still, the sort of day you often get in September. The hills looked yellow in the sunlight, and some smoke was going up a long way off. It was really quiet but from time to time there was a sort of dull booming, like guns being fired miles away.

I suppose it will sound funny, but I felt at peace. I have been feeling like that a lot since everybody went away. I cannot really find the right words to describe it.

When I wake up in the mornings the sun makes a patch low down on the wall by my head, always in the same place. Birds are singing in the trees by the stream and I know if I go to the window the sun will be on the brick wall round the Car Park, and the hills. As it moves round through the day all the shadows change until they point the other way. Sometimes if there is a wind the dust blows across the Car Park in little whirls. When I lock the doors last thing at night the moon is coming up. The moon makes shadows too of course, and they change as well as it goes across the sky. The moonlight makes the Car Park look nearly white but the shadows by the stream are black, like velvet. At night it always seems you can smell the water more clearly. The mist usually comes when it is starting to get light. It makes long streaks that reach as high as the bridge parapet. Nothing else happens. I do not *want* anything else to happen, ever again.

Being on my own was strange at first but I soon got used to it. I was sorry for a while that I would not see Mr Ireland again but I do not think he will come now. I do not think anybody will come.

I have had an odd thought. I think I enjoyed the garden so much when I was small because I could be on my own there. Nobody knew about the secret places except me. I wonder if perhaps that is what I have always wanted. Just to be alone, and not have people always telling me off. Perhaps that is why I wrote so much about the garden, and my pedal car.

The tune about the Lordly Ones has been in my head again all day. There must be a reason for it. I wonder if they are the only people left, if they own everything now. I think it is their fires I can see on the hills.

If they do come, the Stations will be ready. They will see that I have been doing my job.

The water is running again!

It woke me in the night. At first I did not understand, then I could not believe it. The pipes were knocking and banging all round then I heard the big cistern flush, and the hissing as it started to fill again. I got up and went outside. I still could not believe it, but it was true.

I unlocked the Stations and went in with my torch. I was afraid of something overflowing or getting blocked. But everything was working perfectly. I flushed all the cisterns, both sides, again and again; and as fast as I flushed them, they filled back up! It was like a miracle.

I could not go back to sleep. I made some tea instead. As it was a celebration I used the special packet Mr Ireland brought. I even opened some tinned milk I was keeping for a special occasion.

I cannot write any more just now. It is getting light already and I have a lot to do. Both Stations must be cleaned right through, from top to bottom. I expect somebody will be round from the Offices soon, to see how I have been getting on.

I have made another decision. When Mr Ireland comes, I am going to show him what I have written. I expect some of it is silly but I know he will not laugh. I would not show it to anybody else. Nobody in the whole world.

I cannot understand what is happening. The water is still on and the electricity came back this afternoon, I kept trying the switches just in case. But nobody has been to the Stations.

I worked all day. I did everything, the tiles and channels, the pedestals, the downpipes, the windows and floors. I wanted it all to be looking its very best. But nobody came.

I kept telling myself they would be very busy, they would have a lot more important people to see than me. But when it got to evening I started getting anxious again and went up to the telephone box. It was just the same as last time though, the telephone would not answer however much I tried. So I went round to the Offices. They were still shut and big drifts of paper and rubbish had blown up against the doors. So nobody had been there after all.

It was getting late when I came back and I noticed something else. All the hills were dark, there were no fires showing anywhere. So the Lordly Ones have gone away as well.

I do not know what to think. I want to see Mr Ireland again of course but I am getting worried now about all the food still in Mrs Stevens' office. I had to have food if I was going to keep on doing my job but I am afraid if he does come now he will think I took too much. But I did not know how long I would have to be here and it was only spoiling anyway. I did not take anything that was not necessary. I even returned the trolley when I had finished with it, I can show him where I left it. And he will see the water tank and the crane and know I did the best I could.

There have been noises in the town for hours now. Queer noises. It sounds like the shooting again. But that surely cannot be right. It is all over.

I am going to leave the lights on in the Stations tonight, and

the doors unlocked. I know it is against the rules but if there are
people about again someone might need them.

I think maybe the Lordly Ones came down from the hills and
turned the water on for me. I suppose I am really hoping they
will come here. I wonder what they will be like. Beautiful of
course, as it says in the song. I wonder if they will be black.

They have been to the Station!

It was some time during the night, I do not know when. After
I had finished writing I put the office light out and lay down on
the bed. I felt very tired but I did not think I would sleep. I
must have done though because when I opened my eyes again it
was early morning.

I got up at once and went outside. The mist was still hanging
over the brook, the trees looked quite ghostly with it floating
round their trunks. The first thing I noticed was something lying
on the Car Park. It was a piece of cloth, all covered with blood.
There was some more near the Station door. I went inside and
had a nasty shock. There was blood everywhere, on the basins,
on the floor and splashed down one of the walls. So they must
have been badly hurt. If only they had called me! I have bandages
in the office, proper bandages, I brought them back when I
fetched the spare gas cylinders. I could have *helped*.

I got started right away cleaning the mess up. I got it off the
floor and the basins easily enough but it would not come off the
wall, it still left stains however much I rubbed. I wish it had not
gone on the wall but I do not suppose they could help it.

There has been shooting in the town all day. It is still going
on. And there must be a big fire somewhere close because clouds
of smoke keep blowing across the Car Park. The sunlight coming
through it makes it a funny ginger colour. Sometimes I can
hardly see the far wall, and the hills are quite blotted out. I was
going to try and get to the Offices again but I did not dare. I
wish I knew what was going on.

I had a sleep this afternoon. It was only a short nap but I had
a very strange dream. It was as if I was standing a long way off
looking at the Station. It was all on its own in fields, no buildings
near at all, just the big green hills all around. It is still very clear

in my mind. I wish I could draw a picture of it just as I saw it. But I was always very bad at drawing, even at school.

I wish that was how it could be. Just the Station on its own, miles away from anywhere, and me to look after it. I could have a stove for the winter, and curtains I could draw. And I could get up every day and polish the copper pipe under the cistern and do the channels, and the people would come and go from the hills and I could see them. And nothing would change for ever, there would be no more worries at all.

They are here again!

I do not know what the time is. It is still dark. I have lighted a candle to write this, as somehow I did not want to turn the electricity on. I am very nervous, though I am sure there is no need.

Although it is still night I can see the Car Park. There is an orange, flickery light like the light from a bonfire and I can still smell smoke. It must be coming from the burning building.

They are all round the Station. I can hear their feet scuffling and their voices, but I cannot make out what they are saying.

It is silly to be nervous. After all I am not important, they are not interested in me. But if they really are the Lordly Ones, come down from the hills, I am not sure after all that I want to see them.

They are calling something. It sounds like, 'Come out, wherever you are.' That is very strange. They surely cannot mean me.

There is something else now. They are all shouting it together. 'Dan, Dan, the shithouse man.' But that is not right. This is a Comfort Station, and I am its attendant.

This is terrible! They are shooting, at the Station! I can hear the glass going in the windows. They must not do that! It is special glass, I cannot replace it!

There must have been a mistake. They think there is someone else here, someone they do not like. I will go out to them, I should have gone before. I shall blow the candle out first, then open the door. When they see me it will be all right.

I have had a silly thought, the silliest of all. I would like my little car back again now. I always felt safe in it, I could pedal it through the door and they would laugh. They would see I was only a little child after all.

I am putting the light out now.

ARIADNE POTTS

The summer day was still and hot, sunlight pouring from a sky of deepest blue. By the lake edge the air was cooler; so that Henry Potts, who for an hour or more now had tramped dutifully from *Sequoia* to *Castaneus*, from Ilex to Eucalyptus, paused gratefully, producing from his pocket a none-too-white handkerchief with which he proceeded to mop his brow. He had admired the Temple of Flora and the Hermit's Wall, ruminated on the Palladian Bridge and the Gothic Cottage, mused on the distant view of the Pantheon, reflected in the dark green, ruffled waters of the great lake. Now he saw from the guide book he had assiduously purchased that he was approaching the Grotto with its painted leaden Nymph (J. Cheere, attributed.) She looked altogether a most—well, *fetching* Nymph. He eased the strap of the camera round his neck, and wondered if the place would be light enough for a hand-held shot.

Certainly the whole great Estate, claimed by many to contain the finest landscape gardens in the world, had a magical air; Henry, despite his somewhat pedestrian appearance, was by no means insensitive to atmospheres of that kind. He was tallish and thin, inclined to stoop and addicted to the wearing of a peculiarly obnoxious brand of Fair Isle pullovers. He also had a professorial inclination to absent-mindedness, and had been known to turn up on at least one occasion at the small branch Bank in which he had worked for a number of years wearing one of the gaudy garments beneath a business suit. Mr Christopher, the Bank's Manager, had sent him home indignantly to change.

Though pullovers, on this day of days, had for once been discarded. Henry mopped his face again. Really, one could almost say it was a little *too* warm. Loitering here by the water was pleasant enough; but he supposed he should keep walking. No sense in positively *inviting* a chill. Above, a rustic bridge spanned an arm of the lake; he crossed it, smelling the ancient green scent of the water. Tall reeds grew in abundance; over them dragonflies darted and hovered, their wings a chestnut blur above the bright sparks of their bodies. Beyond, stands of hydrangeas, flushed now with a haze of lilac and blue, grew to the water's edge.

The path turned and dipped, presenting changing and unexpected vistas on every side; so that he came on the Grotto suddenly and was surprised by its massiveness and extent. Above it trees grew from traceries of roots that gripped like old gnarled fists; and the path sloped downward sharply, becoming a serpentine walkway flanked by walls of ragged stone.

The chamber he eventually reached was circular, some twelve feet across and constructed of the same ragged blocks. Its floor was of pebbles set in neat concentric rings; an arched opening gave an eye-level prospect of the lake, and a stone church set among trees. To either side were little seats in niches, like the sedilia of a cathedral or church; and at the back of the place, reclining on a moss-grown couch, was the Nymph.

Henry peered. She was a very *realistic* Nymph. Almost uncomfortably so. Her head rested on one firm, well-shaped arm. Her other arm curved behind her on her rocky pillow; and her eyes were lowered, as if she contemplated the crystal spring that rose beneath her couch, poured tinkling and chuckling into a half-round basin before flowing away to feed the waters of the lake. One equally shapely knee was turned, and a little raised; and her bare toes peeped intriguingly from the hem of her robe.

Henry cleared his throat and held a light meter talisman-fashion toward the object of his scrutiny. Sunlight striking through a round hole in the high domed roof of the place caused surprisingly bright reflections. He turned the camera, made adjustments, backed and squinted. He took his picture; then another, and a third. Now, if it was possible from that angle there . . . He circled, crabwise, wheezed a little, concentrated. The click of the camera's metal eye was lost in the lapping echoes of the water. He wound on, closed the flap of the camera case, peered closely once more, sighed and turned away. She was . . . well, not to put too fine a point on it, an *exquisite* Nymph. Henry was not by nature a covetous man; but he would dearly have loved to take her home, have her for his very own.

He stepped away; and a voice behind him said, 'I don't suppose people like you ever think of *royalties* . . .'

He stopped, in consternation and disbelief. For a moment he had almost thought he heard . . . He turned back; and the Grotto spun a little. When it steadied, the Nymph was still regarding him with eyes as brown-green and limpid as the waters of her lake.

Obviously he was suffering some sort of delusion, brought on no doubt by the heat. He leaned on the rough wall of the place, passed a hand over his eyes and shuddered. When he looked again the Nymph was sitting up. 'When you've decided whether or not to *faint*,' she said, 'perhaps you'll help me down off this thing . . .' Her voice had a lilt in it, like the sound of water, and a tiny, not unbecoming lisp. She slid a foot experimentally into the cold crystal of the pool, gathered up her draperies and rose. Henry moved forward, in a species of daze; but the hand she held out to him was firm and cool.

She scuffed down onto the pebbles beside him. She said, 'Thank you.' Her hair, he saw, was brown too, shot through with the most curious glints of greeny-gold; and she was taller than he had realized, by a good three or four inches. He gulped, swallowed and found his voice, though it came out as a sort of croak. He said, 'But you can't . . . I mean it isn't . . .'

She was engaged in drying her ankles, briskly, with the hem of her robe. She said, 'Why not? You *wished* me real. Things like that still do occasionally happen, you know.' She straightened up, in a businesslike way. She said, 'Well, are we ready?'

The Grotto rotated again, and threatened for a moment to black out altogether. Henry said in a species of strangled bleat, 'W-where are you *going?*'

She flicked her hair back. She said, 'With you, of course. I wouldn't be *that* ungrateful.'

Henry had the impression of grasping at straws. 'B-but you *can't!*'

'And why not?'

Henry flapped a hand feebly, bereft once more of words. The Nymph glanced down, and snorted impatiently. She said, 'Oh, *that* . . .' She made swift adjustments to the upper part of her drapery. The result was only a very qualified success. 'If you'd seen some of the things *I've* seen down here recently,' she said bitterly, 'you wouldn't make such a *fuss*. Now for heaven's sake come on . . .'

'W-why are you in such a hurry?'

'If you'd been stuck on that thing for the best part of two hundred years,' she said, pressing ahead, 'you wouldn't *ask* . . .'

A curving way led to another chamber. Presiding over it, with a species of gloomy menace, was the massive, green-stained figure of a River God. The Nymph paused in front of him speculatively. 'It's a good thing you're not bent,' she observed chirpily. 'Imagine being stuck with old Rumbleguts over there . . .'

Beyond the Grotto the path climbed once more, becoming a sunlit stair of rock. At its crest the Pantheon that dominated the lake came abruptly back into sight, huge now and close. The Nymph gazed at it; and her face softened. 'I can remember it being built,' she said. 'It doesn't seem any time at all . . .'

She marched forward purposefully, looking rather like the Primavera minus her daisy chains. Henry pattered at her heels. If curious glances were cast, he was unaware of them; his world was still spinning, in a dissolute sort of way. The Nymph climbed the steps before the Pantheon, pressed herself to the railing that closed off the entrance and stared up at the great white figures inside, cool and still in a flood of pinkish-amber light. 'Goodbye, People,' she said softly.

They had reached the farthest point of the lakeside walk. They crossed a slender bridge that arched above great floating pads of lily leaves. '*Nymphaea Alba*,' observed the Nymph professionally. 'The only indigenous British water lily. Named after me, of course.'

They passed a Cascade, a Rock Bridge, a Hermitage and a Temple of Apollo; and Henry's alarm once more began to verge on the acute. Ahead, close now, were the Scylla of the Tea Rooms, the Charybdis of the Gift Shop, both thronged with folk; and the Nymph's *déshabillé* was once more threatening to become total. But at his muttered presentiment that they were both bound to be arrested she merely tossed her head. 'I'm a life member of the Trust,' she said. 'If there was any justice, I ought to be its *President*. I'd just like to see anybody try!' She stalked past the Tea Rooms, unmolested; she marched past the Gift Shop, undeterred. She stalked into the grassy meadow beyond, where the cars were parked in their bright rows. 'Now,' she said, 'Which is your motor?' Henry glanced back unhappily at the wake of astonishment she had left. He indicated, still speechless, the neat little two-seater that had been his only condescension to the gay life; and she nodded approvingly. 'There's hope yet,' she said. 'You must have hidden depths . . .' She plumped herself down in the passenger seat. 'What's your name, by the way? Mine's Ariadne.'

'Er—Henry Potts!'

The Nymph winced. 'Ariadne Potts . . . Well, I suppose it could be worse . . .'

'Now look here,' said Henry in a species of weak bluster, 'You can't come *home* with me! Not just like that!'

'Why? You're not married or anything boring like that, are you?'

'No, but—'

Ariadne took a pair of sunglasses from the dash cubby, popped them on her short nose. She said, 'Oh, do get *on* with it, Henry. before they find out I'm missing . . .'

'"ART TREASURE STOLEN,"' read Henry over his breakfast marmalade. '"STATUE VANISHES FROM FAMOUS NATIONAL PARK'

'"The theft took place yesterday of a figure of the Nymph Ariadne from the Grotto of the world-famous Stourhead Gardens. Police called to the scene admitted themselves baffled by the robbery, which apparently took place in broad daylight, and are anxious to interview an oddly dressed couple seen in the vicinity sometime in the afternoon . . ."'

'Odd, indeed,' said Ariadne. 'What lousy cheek . . .' She poured tea. 'Pass your cup, Henry, you're going to be late.'

Henry glanced up furtively from behind the paper. One of his pyjama jackets, a trifle overlarge and most casually buttoned, was combining with the Nymph's Classical proportions to do the most alarming things to his pulse rate. Ariadne buttered toast composedly. She said, 'You'll have to leave me some money on the way, to buy some more clothes. I'll use that old pair of jeans we found for shopping, and one of your woollies. Then I'll do something about that larder of yours. Honestly, nothing but stuff in *cans* . . .'

Henry said weakly, 'H-how much will you want?'

'Sixty or seventy pounds should do for a start. No, make it seventy if I'm doing the housekeeping. Then we'll see.'

Henry swallowed. 'I haven't got that much in the house!'

'Then I'll stop by at the Bank for it. You'd better open us a joint account by the way, so I shan't have to come pestering you all the time.'

'I can't do that!'

'Why on earth not?'

Henry waved his hands desperately. 'You haven't got any papers. You need papers to get papers. You don't even *exist!*'

The Nymph took a breath, and fixed him with a steely stare. 'After last night,' she said, 'I can only say I'm surprised at you, Henry Potts!'

Henry capitulated. The night had indeed been the most interesting, though undeniably the most hectic, of his life.

Ariadne nodded, in a satisfied sort of way. 'That's all right then,' she said calmly. 'You can tell them at the Bank you just met me and married me. *Splot*, just like that. It only takes two minutes in a Registry Office anyway. And papers aren't any problem. If we need them we'll just forge a few. It should be easy, with all your photography and whatnots.'

Henry choked; and the Nymph began composedly stacking plates. 'You'd better see about an Access card as well, by the way,' she said. 'With inflation running at twenty-six per cent you can positively *make* money on them. I'll see you later on.'

Henry rose hurriedly. 'Look,' he said, 'don't come round to the bank. I'll slip back, midmorning. Mr Christopher won't mind, if I'm quick.'

'OK then,' said Ariadne. 'See you do . . .' Then, catching sight once more of the clock, 'Darling, you'll have to *fly*. Don't forget your hat . . .'

Henry scurried for the door; but the Nymph called him back. He stood uncertainly, his hat in his hands; and she put up her cheek, demurely. 'Kiss me goodbye,' she said. 'It's customary, with husbands . . .'

Henry's return visit to the flat later that morning disclosed no sign of Ariadne. The sitting room was empty; in the diminutive kitchen the breakfast crockery was back in its cupboard, the sink tidied, the dishcloth folded neatly on the draining board. Everything looked perfectly normal. He called uncertainly, pushed open the doors of bedroom and loo. Nobody. So that was that then; it had been a delusion all along. An impulse made him check the morning paper. He found it folded where he always left it, on the sideboard in the sitting room. The item about the theft at Stourhead was definitely there. So at least he hadn't dreamed that part. Odd that he should have been there himself at the time. But coincidences did happen. Perhaps it would be an idea to slip round to the doctor's though, later on, have a chat with him about it. He might be able to give him something for it.

A little self-consciously, he left the brown envelope with the money on the sideboard. It had all cleared itself up, as he had expected all along; it might even turn out to have a perfectly natural explanation. But there was no point in taking chances.

All the same, his work at the Bank suffered badly. He found himself dreaming over his ledgers and statements; twice Mr Christopher snapped at him in passing. The most persistent of the images that floated between him and the neatly-drawn totals was that of a face with eyes as golden-green as lake water, lips that parted to reveal regular pearly little teeth.

At lunchtime, as was his custom, he betook himself to a small pub set back a few yards from the busy High Street. It was quiet since they had declared the town centre a Pedestrian Precinct; almost like a little plaza, with bright-coloured sunshades set above pavement tables. He bought himself a Ploughman's and a half of bitter, sat a little furtively listening to the clittering of high heels on flags. Girls in plenty thronged the town, girls in bright summer frocks; but not like Ariadne. Nor did she appear as he finished his snack, made his way back to his place of toil.

By three-thirty, when the Bank doors were closed and the last of the customers ushered out, he had wholly accepted the notion that she had been nothing more than a figment of his imagination. He had decided against a trip to the surgery; but he would have to watch himself in the future. He couldn't afford to go round getting figments just like that, not at his time of life. It wasn't respectable. He finished his totting-up and drove home, let himself into the little first-floor flat. He couldn't decide, on balance, whether to be pleased or not.

The Nymph's welcome knocked him fully halfway across the small hall. He recovered himself, gasping; and Ariadne pirouetted in front of him. 'I found the most *adorable* little boutique,' she said. 'What do you think, isn't it great?'

Henry didn't answer. 'It' consisted of a sort of frilly blouse-top thing, tied up high under her breasts; it was worse, if anything, than the Classical Drape. A pair of tight, appallingly-pink trousers gave up an admittedly unequal task at a point no self-respecting garment should; while on her feet were arty little sandals, all folk weave and thongs.

'And this,' said Ariadne. 'And there . . .' Skirts and dresses, another blouse, bright red cloggy with-it shoes. 'They'd got a gorgeous little bikini,' said the Nymph happily. 'In a sort of goldy-brown, just my colour. But I ran a bit short, I shall have to go back. Still, I didn't do badly. Fifty-eight, twenty-three and a half. I got a bill . . .'

She danced through to the kitchen. Henry tottered after her. The place looked as if a cyclone had hit it. Shelves had been emptied, cupboards turned out; the 'fridge was defrosting mess-ily, and cartons and carrier bags stood about everywhere, 'I threw out all those rotten old teabags,' said Ariadne. 'I don't know how you can drink that stuff. I got us some proper tea instead. The kettle's on, it won't be a minute.' She started arranging dishes. 'I bought some new saucepans too. Look, don't you think they're gorgeous . . . What we really need is a deepfreeze of course. I thought everybody had one.'

Tea consisted of a deftly-prepared salad; mounds of lettuce, radishes, carrots and apples diced and tossed in a delicious oil. When it was over the Nymph bounced on to Henry's still-astonished lap. Up close, she smelled of some faint, delicious scent. 'That's water hawthorn,' she said. 'Things happen after a Whotsit's Bath; or didn't you know?' She tickled him. 'You breathe in horses' nostrils to make them trust you,' she said. 'What do you think would happen if I blew down your ear . . . ?'

★

She was up a clear half hour before him in the morning, pattering round the kitchen. Delicious smells met Henry as he trudged from the bathroom. 'In the normal course of things,' said Ariadne sternly, 'I don't hold with fried food. But you need some tallow on you, Henry Potts.' She slid crisp bacon rashers onto a warmed plate, followed them with an egg like a sunburst. 'You'd think,' she said, 'with all that *stodge* you'd got there, you'd be like a balloon. But there's nothing *to* you!' She giggled, happily. 'Leastways, not exactly. But you know what I mean . . .'

On his way to the Bank, Henry found himself positively beaming; at the town, the streets, the folk that thronged them on their way to work. And surely too the sky was bluer, the engine of the little car ran sweeter than he could remember for many a year. His hours of rest, once more, had been hours of revelation. One moment in particular he savoured, rolling it round his mind like an aftertaste round the tongue. 'Turn over, darling,' Ariadne had whispered, 'and I'll show you how the ancient Romans used to do it . . .' So her Classical education, as she had proved, was sound in all departments.

With regard to the Nymph herself, he had given up a thoroughly one-sided struggle. If she *was* a continuing figment of his imagination, then his imagination was fertile enough to be wholly satisfying; while if her entry into his life was the portent of some appalling psychological disorder he had decided, quite straightforwardly, that he didn't want to be cured. He bounced into the Bank; he beamed at the customers; he beamed at Mr Christopher and at old Miss Peabody, who had been his arch-enemy for years. He even beamed at the pretty little new assistant, who had previously considered 'that Mr Potts' a rather dry old stick, accompanying his beam with what the astonished girl was later only able to construe as a wink. His work thrived; and he hummed his way homeward once more well content.

The sight that met his eyes was if anything more alarming than that of the evening before. His wardrobe and chest of drawers, the pegs in the hall, had been stripped; clothes, old and not so old, were scattered in heaps; and on the largest stack, ominously ticketed 'JUMBLE SALE', he saw his entire stock of pullovers. He wailed, rushing to their rescue; but the Nymph forestalled him. She was lounged in a chair, a fat catalogue in her lap, looking cool and elegant in a linen shirtwaister dress that surely hadn't been among her purchases of the day before. 'Henry,' she said, 'don't you *dare* . . . Come over here and kiss me instead.'

Henry obliged, contritely; but to his protests that the offending garments would 'do for messing about in', the Nymph turned a deaf ear. 'The only messing about you'll be doing in future,' she said, 'will be with me. And you're *not* doing it in a Fair Isle jumper. Now, what's your Inside Leg?'

The catalogue, she explained, would serve till the next sales came round; she had conned it out of a perfectly dear Collector who called at the downstairs flat. The meeting also explained the provenance of the new dress. To her dissertation on the importance of personal image in the modern world Henry, who had never really thought about the matter before, made no demur. Events had already passed him at the gallop.

'And there's another thing,' said the Nymph over supper—a candlelit meal with avocado starters. 'While I was clearing some drawers out in the back, I found these.' She whacked down, before Henry's startled gaze, his Bank and Building Society pass books. 'Do you,' she said, 'have any serious idea what you're *worth?*'

Henry was a careful man, and in fact had a very exact idea. His parents' deaths had left him, though not wealthy, at least comfortably endowed; though his father, with the inexplicable pique of the elderly, had insisted at the last moment on the sale of the family house and furniture, necessitating his removal to the flat. He stammered something to that effect; but the Nymph cut him short. 'Then why on *earth*,' she said impatiently, 'are you scratching along in a poky little dump like *this?*'

Henry attempted to set out his views on the inadvisability of Breaking into Capital; but his peroration was equally shortlived. 'With inflation like this country's got,' said Ariadne, 'capital is just so much money down the *drain*.' She poured a glass of well-chilled *Liebfraumilch*. Henry felt the delicate fumes rise instantly to his brain.

'Now let's just see,' said the Nymph. She figured rapidly. 'We needn't pay all cash of course . . . so three times your annual salary, put down say nine . . . we could go up to fifteen, we could get quite a decent place for that. Least, it would do for a *start* . . .'

Henry wailed, appalled at the instant vision that had come to him of Estate Agents and Searches and Surveys and Exchanges of Contracts. 'But mortgage rates are running at twelve per cent!'

'Less five for tax relief,' corrected the Nymph. 'And where else could you borrow money at seven per cent? Henry, you can't afford *not* to!'

'B-but . . .'

'What now? You do make difficulties!'

'I don't *like* Estate Agents!' It was the way they looked at you, sort of sizing you up; and they were always going round gazumping and such, doing things that were Darker than Night.

'Leave the Estate Agents to me,' said Ariadne calmly. 'Is there an evening paper round here?'

'Only the Echo . . .'

'Then get one tomorrow, on your way home. And I'll start doing the rounds. The sooner we get moving, the better!'

'Please, Henry,' said Ariadne much later, '*won't* you do it? Not even for *me*?' She sat up beside him, her hair tousled with moonlight, and turned on him the huge pools of her eyes.

'And that,' said the Nymph, 'is all there is to it. I need it; it's an essential, so we shall just have to put up with it. Look on it as an investment.'

But . . . Collyer, Son and Partners, the longest-established and most exclusive saddlers and outfitters in the district! Collyers, still ensconced in the High Street of Midchester, whose emporium breathed out an air of leather and sanctity onto the uninitiated . . . Henry attempted, feebly, to compute the cost of a complete riding outfit from them, and gave up. 'If you'd only go somewhere cheaper . . .'

'I am *not*,' said Ariadne coldly, 'putting myself up in a badly-fitting *jacket* . . .'

'But you don't even *like* horses! Not all that *much!*'

'I agree they aren't quite my image,' said the Nymph composedly. 'And I always felt there was something wrong-side-of-the-blanket about the Centaurs anyway. But that's not the point. It isn't for me, it's for Mr Vanderkloss. The *senior* Mr Vanderkloss . . .'

'That old crook!' howled Henry. 'He's the biggest twister in town!'

'I agree he's mature,' said the Nymph distantly. 'But as a matter of fact he's perfectly *sweet*. And he *adores* riding.'

'But half the stuff he handles doesn't even have roofs! When you're in my position, you hear things!'

'You aren't *in* a position,' said Ariadne crushingly. 'Not as yet anyway. As for his property list, *I* happen to know there's a very nice Detached indeed coming on the market soon. Twenty seven foot lounge, patio, three bedrooms, bathroom and fitted kitchen, separate loo, recently modernized, gas CH. throughout . . .'

'It's out of the question . . .'

'Garage, mature garden,' said the Nymph dreamily. 'Secluded position on No Through Road, fitted carpets optional. Not that we shall *want* them of course, they're bound to be appalling . . .'

'They'll want twenty thousand!'

'They might *want* it,' said the Nymph, looking demure. 'But Mr Vanderkloss is going to discover the most *appalling* attack of Dry Rot . . .' She slid snakily onto Henry's lap, twined her arms round his neck. 'I don't like it when you're cross,' she whispered. 'Let's go to bed . . .'

The following day, a Saturday, saw Henry driving complainingly to Midchester, decanting a delighted Nymph—she had chosen sober, spectacularly-tailored tweeds for the expedition, and was looking about as County as it was possible to get—on the hallowed doorstep of Mr Collyer, his Son and Partners. A few days and the loss of his moustache later ('Grow your *hair* instead,' Ariadne had said) he drove, equally protestingly, to the riding stables of her choice, parked outside the tall red-brick gatepillars with their imposing ornamental lanterns. 'You'd better not come inside,' said Ariadne thoughtfully. 'You're not *quite* ready yet, we can't have you frightening the horses.' She tickled his ear playfully with her crop, and was gone.

Henry watched her striding away from him up the drive of the place. Her boots, her cap, her breeches were immaculate, the fit of her jacket a thing to marvel at; her hair, drawn into a severe Classical bob, set off to perfection the swanlike grace of her neck and throat, where floated a wisp of bright chiffon. The expression on his face was curious. In part, certainly, it was one of admiration; in part, regrettably, of lust; but there was also something else, that seemed quite alien to him.

Within what seemed to Henry an indecently short span of time an offer for the place had been made and accepted; searches had been completed, inspections carried out and contracts exchanged. A small army of workmen had descended, banging that which was bangable, tapping that which was tappable and painting almost everything; but now they too were gone.

'And the beauty of it is,' said the Nymph, wielding a tack-hammer enthusiastically, 'it will all be yours one day. Paying *rent* gets you *nowhere* . . .' She sat back on her heels. 'There, doesn't it look *great?*'

Henry turned, slightly startled, from a contemplation of her expanse of jean-clad bottom. The long room, west-facing, was lit by the rays of the setting sun. French doors stood ajar; beyond were lawns and rockeries, a shrub garden, a fishpond where a little fountain played. The plaster gnomes that had been dis-covered infesting it had been conveyed by Ariadne, tight-lipped, to the dustbin. Henry lay back negligently in one of the big deep leather-covered chairs discovered by the Nymph in Midchester Antiques—the owner, mysteriously, had halved the price on the sale tickets—and regarded his new domain. The money already paid out had kept him from what remained of his sleep for weeks; but that was in the past now too. A pipe was between his lips, a decanter and soda syphon on the table at his side; and it seemed the world had never before been quite such a capital place.

The Nymph walked to him, soundless on bare feet, curled herself on the arm of the chair. She said, 'Your hair's growing nicely now. And ooh *look*, Henry, it's *curling!* You're beginning to look most distinguished . . .'

Henry pinched her, with the ease of long familiarity. She giggled and retaliated. The wrestling match that ensued landed them both on the floor. Henry sat up puffing. 'Mind the Scotch. No, *mind!*'

He pushed the hair out of his eyes. He said, 'Y'know, Ary, I've been thinking.'

'Hmmm . . . Don't think. Let's go and look at the shrubbery again.'

'No, listen. That job I was talking about. Assistant Manager in the Midchester branch. I was thinking of having a go for it.'

'What does Mr Christopher say?'

'Doesn't think I've got a chance.'

'Hmpph. Boo to him. *I'll* come and see him if he doesn't watch it.'

She sat up frowning.

'What's the matter? Don't you think I'd get it either?'

The Nymph tossed her head. ''*Course* you would! It wasn't that. It's just . . .' She put her head on one side, considered. 'Assistant Manager. Then Branch Manager. Hmm . . .'

'What's the matter?'

'It sounds so . . . sort of humdrum. You're worth better!'

Henry said, 'It's a good secure position.'

She wrinkled her nose. 'You know what I think about that!'

'Well, you have to allow for these things.'

'I have done,' said Ariadne. 'I was secure for long enough. It doesn't bear thinking about . . .' Then her eyes widened, and she grasped his arm. 'Henry, I *forgot!* I haven't even *seen* them yet!'

'W-what?'

'Your photographs,' said the Nymph. 'The ones I *have* seen are super. You could make a *fortune!*'

Henry said, 'If I've told you once I've told you a dozen times . . .' But she was already rushing about, closing curtains, switching on wall lights, setting up screens. 'Quick,' she said. 'Get the projector . . .'

The fan of the little Aldis roared companionably. Henry worked the slide carrier; and the Nymph, her arms draped companionably across his knees, took her thumb from her mouth. She said, '*Gosh* . . .'

He had shown her, first, his collection of flower studies. The boxes in which he kept them were tidily labelled. British (Wild), Horticultural, Exotic; Roses (Shrub), (Climbing) and (Tea). Then his canal pictures, the views he had taken on his one trip to Scotland. 'Seascapes, Various' followed; then birds and animals, dogs, Domestic and Church Architecture. He had had a passion, at one time, for fonts; they too had acquired a special category. Ariadne had 'oohed' with pleasure, 'Aahed' with uncertainty; and finally lapsed into silence. So he had turned to the boxes he kept a little apart from the rest. 'Garden Statuary of Britain . . .' His hand hesitated over them, a natural delicacy holding him back; but if the Nymph remembered her own origins she paid no heed. From the very first transparency, her attention was riveted. The 'Oohs' and 'Aahs' returned, in crescendo; finally she leaped up. 'Henry,' she said, 'you're a genius!'

'Oh,' he said modestly, 'I wouldn't say that. Look, there's loads more yet.'

She settled back. 'Show me them all!'

He complied. Across the screen passed the mermen and conch-blowing Tritons, the dolphins and dragons, the cupids and Herakles of the eighteenth century fancy; and girls with laurel wreaths, boys with poodles, Gods and Queens and fisherboys, monkeys and chimaeras, horsemen and lions; and finally of course, the Nymphs. They had been his secret passion for years. Nymphs in sunlight, Nymphs in dappled green shade; Nymphs at dawn and in shadowed dusk, rain-wet Nymphs glistening against dark grey skies. Nymphs who ran and danced, Nymphs who lounged beside cool pools; Nymphs who wore gowns of Classical loveliness, Nymphs who wore chaplets of flowers and fruit, Nymphs who wore nothing at all. 'Look at *that* one,' Ariadne said. 'She's just like me . . .' Oh and that one, she's *gorgeous* . . . Henry, that's really *naughty!* No, please go back, I want another *look* . . .'

It was the small hours before the show was finished; and Henry turned the room lights on, switched off the projector lamp and left it to blow itself cool. The Nymph bustled about in the kitchen, making coffee and bits and pieces. She said, 'They're *marvellous*. It was like a sort of trip . . .'

Nobody had ever seen Henry's collection before. Nobody had ever wanted to. He started coiling leads away. He said, 'There's some good *compositions* there.'

'Compositions, my foot,' shouted the Nymph from the galley. 'They're sexy, every one, they're fizzing with it. You've got a sort of eye for it . . .'

Henry started folding up the screen. 'I wouldn't say that . . .'

'I don't think you can even *see* it! They had me going up the wall!'

Henry said severely, 'That's *enough*, Ariadne!' But she was not to be put down. 'I told you we hadn't started,' she said, setting down plates and cups. 'Now I'll prove it. I'm going to London!'

Henry groaned. 'It's no use, I've told you before. I've had my name on the books with half a dozen Agencies for years. It's all syndicated, all that sort of stuff. Amateurs don't get a look in.'

'You haven't got "all that sort of stuff." Yours is different! and you didn't have *me* to sell it before!'

'You'll be wasting your time.'

'There is always a market,' said the Nymph primly, 'for sophisticated eroticism. People get fed up with the other sort.' She sucked her thumb again, thoughtfully. 'I shall need some new outfits of course,' she said. 'You know how I feel about Image.'

Henry spluttered over his coffee. 'You had three new dresses last week!'

'I can't go to London in *those!*' And I can't wear *tweeds*. They'd think I was up from the country . . . And we'd better buy a new projector as well, an automatic. So I can keep on talking while they're going through. It'll be an investment . . .'

Henry groaned. 'But they cost *hundreds* . . .'

Ariadne came and tucked herself down by his feet, huddling up very small. She put her arms on his knees, and stared up steadily with her great eyes. 'The last time I made an investment,' she said, 'we got this house. Don't you trust me *yet?*'

The Nymph looked over the tops of the flyaway hornrim glasses she now sometimes affected. Her vision, actually, was as near twenty/twenty as made no odds; but she claimed they gave her a more mature, responsible air. 'The Observer are talking about another series,' she said. 'The money isn't too bad but the agent says to hold out, he thinks he can get more. And he still says Playboy are definitely interested. With devaluation bonus that ought to be worth at least two thousand a shot. Less commission, say fifteen hundred. Oh and there's another calendar commission in, I've already accepted that. "A Nymph throughout the seasons." Just one girl. It'll be different.'

Henry said, 'Who are we using?'

She lowered her eyes. 'Me, actually. I thought it would save on model fees. What do you want to do about the Observer?'

'Better do as he says. He's been right most times so far.'

The typewriter clattered. Ariadne said 'Damn' and back-spaced. She said, 'What we really need is another machine. This one's clapped. Particularly if we're going to have a go at that other thing we talked about.'

Henry said, 'I really think we've got enough on our hands at the moment, my dear.'

He was sitting, crossed legs stuck out, very much at ease in a fawn sweater and fawn, knife-creased slacks. His hair, curling elegantly about his ears, was touched with a silver that gave him added dignity. He was going through the page proofs of his latest book, 'Exotic Journey.' (Illustrations by the well known photographer Henry Potts, text by his wife Ariadne). His first book, 'Living Ornaments,' had hit the somewhat staid market of the high-price glossies like a small bomb, and had run to an unbelievable six editions; it had enabled him to pay off his mortgage, and they were looking for another place already. One of the results of its publication, a popular cult of Garden Nymphs, had grown till it finally attracted the attention of the media; and Henry, with unprecedented acumen, had acquired a controlling interest in a small run-down manufactory on the outskirts of Midchester, which was now busily engaged turning out fibreglass copies of his most famous subjects for export to places as far removed as California and Hong Kong. Ariadne, showing hitherto-unsuspected skills, had designed a series of what she called Exciting Birdbaths, to be produced in the same material; and they were selling like hot cakes too. The future looked decidedly rosy.

The Nymph took her glasses off and yawned. She walked across to Henry, plucked the galleys out of his hands and threw them on the table. She said, 'You've done enough of that old stuff for one day. Make room for *me*.' She kissed his ear, and started twirling with his hair. She said, 'I want to talk about *our* book.'

Henry protested. 'You know I can't write *novels* . . .'

'You don't have to. I'll dictate it to you. It'll be a smash hit, you know how popular romantic fiction is.'

'It's still a new field. I reckon we should stick to what we know.'

'Diversification,' carolled Ariadne, 'is the springboard of commercial success. Anyway, it can't miss, not with what *I* shall put in it. I was there you see. I *really* know what happened. The material's endless. And some of the goings-on you just wouldn't *believe* . . .'

Henry reached for his whisky; but she trapped his arm. She said, 'I shan't *let* you. Not till you say yes . . .'

'You'll have the chair over in a minute!'

'Say *yes!*'

'Oh, very well. If it will keep you quiet.'

She kissed him. 'You're a *darling* . . . And can I have a new typewriter then? *Please* . . .'

'I suppose so . . .'

The Nymph said, '*Mmmmm* . . .' She sat up, regarding Henry solemnly. She said, 'I *knew* you'd say yes. So as a matter of fact . . .'

He narrowed his eyes. He said, 'I'm waiting.'

She hung her head. She said, 'Well, I sort of *saw* one. The other day, in Midchester. It was just what we wanted . . .'

Henry said, '*Where is it?*'

'In your study. It's a beauty. Honest, you'll love it. Henry, *wait* . . .'

But he had already plunged through the door. A moment later a howl of anguish rent the air. 'An IBM . . . six hundred bloody quid's worth . . .'

She ran to him. But Henry, for the first time, had thoroughly lost his temper. He pointed a trembling finger at the monster that had invaded his study. 'It goes straight *back* . . .'

'It can't! I paid half cash down!'

Henry howled afresh. 'We're up to here already. *Here*, I tell you. Now this . . . this . . .'

'But it's all deductible. And it isn't our money anyway, it's only the Company's. It's an expendable asset!'

'Sometimes,' fumed Henry, 'as far as the Company's concerned, *I* seem to be an expendable asset!'

'Don't talk nonsense! Everything I've done's been for you!'

Henry ticked off on his fingers. 'I used to sleep at nights. Now my ulcers are growing ulcers. I used to have a nine-to-five. Now I work all hours God sends . . .'

'You're just *ungrateful!*'

'All I'm trying to do is get us back in the black . . .'

'But we don't *want* to be in the black! We'll get *taxed!*'

'Last week I almost managed it . . .'

'I know! That's why we had to have the Volvo!'

'We had to have the Volvo,' bellowed Henry, 'because you nagged and nagged till it nearly drove me *spare!*'

'I *didn't* nag! I *never* nag! I was only thinking of what was best!'

'You know it all, don't you . . .'

The Nymph faced him, breasts heaving. 'Sometimes, I think I do! And so far, Henry Potts, I haven't been too far *wrong!* Look what you were when I found you! A tatty little man working in a Bank!'

'Don't you call me a tatty little man!'

'I *didn't!* I'm *not!*'

Henry took a deep breath. He said with exaggerated patience, 'All I want, is a say in what my own firm does. Just now and then. Is that being too unreasonable?'

'You're the one who's being unreasonable! You do get a say, every time!'

'Then what about *that?*'

The Nymph drew herself up. She said, 'That was different. You'd have said no. Now, you can't. I've made an investment!'

'The next time I hear that word,' said Henry, blowing through his nostrils like an overworked horse, 'I will not be responsible for my actions . . .'

'*Investment! Investment!*'

Henry said, '*That's it* . . .' He made a flying grab for the Nymph, who eeled back out of reach. The slammed door held him up for vital seconds; he almost caught her at the foot of the stairs, but she slipped past him again. He skid-turned into the lounge. Furniture crashed, a standard lamp went flying. He

pinned her finally, with a species of flying tackle. She squalled
and writhed; he rolled her across his knee regardless, and
spanked until his shoulder ached. When he paused for breath
she was still wriggling, making little mewing noises to herself.
'Henry,' she said, 'you're so *masterful*, you've never done *anything*
like that before. Don't stop . . .'

'"*The God in the Garden*,"' read the Nymph, '"the latest from
the pen of that remarkable storyteller Henry Potts, is in the
opinion of this reviewer his best novel to date. Potts' spicy sagas
show an insight into the doings of the eighteenth century, both
great and humble, that is one of the literary phenomena of our
time; while his clear-cut imagery and incisive style are only to be
expected from one who, before turning to the written word, had
already made an international reputation as a photographer of
Stately Homes, and the curious and frequently exotic inhabitants
of their grounds . . ."'

She put the paper down. 'The clippings agency sent about a
dozen more reviews this morning,' she said. 'They're all pretty
good. And the publishers wrote to say they're reprinting "*The
Lost Nymph*" again. How many impressions is that?'

'I don't know,' said Henry shortly. 'Eight or ten. It doesn't
make much difference.'

The Nymph looked at him reproachfully. Success had changed
him somehow. His manner was harsher, more abrupt; and he
had taken to drinking a good deal more than was good for him.
His answer, invariably, was that it was his money and he could
spend it how he chose. If he bought malt whisky by the crate, it
was his own affair.

The breakthrough had finally come with the Playboy contract.
Their gatefold series, live girls posed against their stone and
metal counterparts, had been simple enough in conception; but
Henry's camera had once more worked its magic. Afterwards a
calendar had been produced that had acquired an international
notoriety second only to that recently enjoyed by the firm of
Pirelli. The little company in Midchester had likewise expanded,
introducing a new line of figures cast from living models; and
Henry's reputation had finally been assured by a writ for
obscenity served on him by a well-known and noble do-gooder.

The resulting publicity had assured the Company work for many months to come; and Henry had diversified again, taking under his control a firm of landscape architects and another that specialized in the supply of decorative building stone. After that the Potts, now with an entourage that included a secretary, a cook-housekeeper and a full time gardener, had removed themselves to more distinguished surroundings; Henry looked down now from the first floor windows of a not inconsiderable eighteenth century manor house, onto an immaculate sweep of lawns and gravelled drives. Beside the Volvo Estate, still used for Henry's photographic jaunts abroad, stood a big Mercedes; farther along the creeper-hung frontage was parked Ariadne's old but much-loved XKE. A peacock strutted importantly on the terrace; beyond, over the wall that enclosed the grounds, the tops of cars and lorries moved silently like manifestations from another world.

Henry sloshed whisky negligently into a glass. He said, 'I shall have to go to Germany again next week, probably Tuesday. Finish that job for Sondermann Verlag. I shall probably be gone about ten days.'

The Nymph said softly, 'Oh, no . . .'

He turned to her irritably. The day had been sultry, sticky; thunder was in the offing, and the evening air had brought no relief. He said, 'I can't put it off any longer. And we need the money. We don't live in a three and a half room flat any more; or hadn't you noticed?'

She didn't answer; and he drank, set the glass down, poured himself another. She walked to him, tried to slip onto his lap; but he pushed her aside. He said wearily, 'Not again . . . It's your answer to everything, isn't it?'

She stood aside, quietly. She said, 'It's just that I don't like to see you unhappy.'

'I'm *not* unhappy! And I doubt frankly if *that* ever entered your mind . . .' He drummed his fingers. 'Oh, for God's sake leave me alone. Don't stand there *staring*. Just give me some peace, can't you? It isn't much to ask . . .'

She said, 'Shall I go away?'

'Yes. No. Oh, do what you like. I don't care . . .'

She didn't speak, and he in turn didn't move his head; but he knew she hadn't left the room. He knew too, from experience, the expression that would be on her face; the dumb reproach, the animal hurt in the big wide eyes. It was a trick, like all the rest, a trick to get her own way. She had tricked him all the time; no direction he had ever taken had truly been his, no decision he had made had been his own. He knew her now too well. He knew that in the night to come, the hot, sticky night, she would snuggle up to him; he knew the tricks she would use to rouse him, the posturings, the pretended resistance, the equally make-believe submission. '*Hurt me,*' she would whisper. 'Please hurt me . . .' She, the unhurtable. Sometimes now he thought back almost with longing, to the old days at the Bank; Miss Peabody's acrid morning smiles, Mr Christopher's gruff and predictable complaints. He wondered why he had ever desired Ariadne, and her alone. Her body was like ten thousand other bodies, ten million. No better, and no worse. He should know; he had seen enough of them, over the years. Except, perhaps, that hers would never age.

She said in a small voice, 'Henry . . .'

'What is it *now?*'

She said, 'I . . . wouldn't mind. Honestly. If you went away. With . . . some of the others. You could get them now. I'd still be here when you came back . . .'

He turned to face her slowly. He said, '*What?*'

She hung her head. She said, 'I can thought-read. I always could. I'm sorry . . .'

He said, 'If that isn't the last bloody *straw* . . .' He flung the glass away. It broke. He felt, quite suddenly, the need to hurt her; make, her, just for once, *feel*. It was a need he had felt before; and put from him, unaccepted. 'There used,' he said, 'to be a grand old-fashioned word. Privacy. But it doesn't seem to exist now. Not any more . . .'

Most certainly, the whisky had got to him; but it was too late to care. He heard his own voice dimly, shouting; and some of her answers.

'You've been smarter than I have all along, haven't you? You've always been smart. Is that why you latched on to me in the first place? Because you thought you could work me, twist me round your finger? Well, *is it?*'

'It wasn't like that! It wasn't like that at all!'

'You were laughing at me!'

'*No!*'

'Don't lie to me! You thought I didn't know! Well, I do know! I know everything I need to!'

She was talking again, or mumbling. He said incredulously, '*What?*'

'I . . . it doesn't matter. I only said . . . that I forgive you. After all, you're only a mortal . . .'

'Why, you cheeky little—'

She was shaking her head, like a pony trying to get away from flies. She said, 'It doesn't matter. Not any more. I thought . . . but it's all right . . .'

'Doesn't matter?' shouted Henry, beside himself. '*Doesn't matter?* You stand there and patronize me, then tell me it doesn't matter . . . !'

She seemed to be having trouble speaking. 'I . . . thought you were different. That's all. Kind. But you're . . . all the same really, when it comes down to it . . .'

'Meaning you're tired of me!'

'I'm not!'

'You don't want me! You never did!'

She stamped her foot. 'Not like *this* I don't!'

'Well, I don't want you! I—' He stopped and she stared at him, fists clenched. 'Go on, Henry,' she said. 'Say it . . .'

Henry swallowed. 'I wish,' he said, slowly, driving the words between his teeth like daggers, '*that you'd never come to life . . .*'

An odd thing happened. She swung away, spun round as if hit by some physical blow. She stood a moment, shoulders hunched; then she turned back. 'Henry,' she said, 'have you ever seen a statue cry? Then take a good, hard look . . .' She ran from the room. He heard her feet on the stairs; then the door slammed shut behind her.

He sat a moment in stunned silence. Then realization dawned. He shouted, *Ariadne . . . !*

He ran for the stairs, the Great Hall. But he was too late. Gravel splashed outside; he ran again, glimpsed the red tail of the Jaguar vanishing through the high stone gateposts of the drive. He flung himself at the Merc, scrabbled the door undone.

The gateposts veered past him; he hauled at the wheel, hauled straight again, pushed his foot down to the floor. But fast as he drove, the low red car moved faster.

The daylight faded. He glimpsed the Jag again, twice; on the main road junction, and on the motorway approach beyond. Then it was lost in the jewel-strings of tail lights that flashed down endlessly, into the still-bright west. He took the Mercedes to a hundred and beyond, cutting recklessly from lane to lane. Headlights flashed behind him; horns yelled indignantly, but he paid no heed. Of the red car, there was no sign. Fifty miles on he pulled onto the hard shoulder, sat trembling, drinking in great gulps of warm night air. He wiped his face and the rim of the wheel, set himself to drive again.

It was past midnight before he reached his destination; but the night, that had been velvet-black, was no longer so. Thunder grumbled and crashed, lightning danced a great pink flickering dance above the clouds. The reflections showed him the shuttered Gift Shop, the shuttered Tea Rooms, glanced from the still expanse of the lake beyond. By the railings that fenced the place off, its cockpit empty, stood the XKE.

He skidded the Mercedes to a halt, left the door swinging. The entrance turnstiles were chained and padlocked; he vaulted them and began to run. The lightning blazed again, showed him vasts mounds of velvet that were the stands of trees. He shouted again, his voice thin and lost. '*Ariadne . . .*'

The temples by the lake edge stared, with faces of tilted bone. He reached the rustic bridge, stumbled across. The path turned and dipped; he ran again, lost his footing and rolled. A water bird erupted from the lake; he sat up breathing harshly and the storm broke, with a flash and peal. Rain hissed into the lake in drenching curtains, poured down through the leaves of the great gnarled trees.

And there was the descending path, the humped shape of the Grotto. He stumbled, hands to the rough walls, feeling the cold air breathe from ahead. His own shout roared from the cavern, mixed with the thunder voice. He splashed knee-deep into the cistern; he flung his hands out, groping blind, and touched a figure of painted lead.

SPHAIRISTIKE

It's one of the more curious traits of the human race that the greater the marvels it's offered, the quicker it tires of them. I've read for instance that in the earliest days of space exploration folk got bored at a positively breakneck pace, took to turning their videoscreens back to the endless, mindless quizzes we still enjoy and moaning at the air time wasted on yet another earthman ambling about the moon. Certainly the first holographic transmissions were almost literally a nine day wonder. After the usual beggar-your-neighbour rush to buy the new gear, the family feuds just carried on in sitting rooms around the globe; the singers and dancers strutting between the combatants were dismissed as little more than background interference. So it's no surprise that Synths, now they've become a commonplace, are no more regarded than the rest. Except of course when van Mechelren, the High Court whizz kid, throws one of his periodic junketings; and brings the name of InterNatMech once more, briefly, before the public eye. But of course the one thing that has never palled is scandal in high places.*

Maybe I'm being a little unfair; certainly there's no real reason any of you should recall the name of Col Lowston, professional *enfant terrible* and darling of the media. Particularly as his high time goes back to the last millennium; the Nasty Nineties, as they came to be known. I remember him well, from the days when he was a bouncy undergrad; irritating, charming when he chose to be and with too much brain for anybody else's good, as one of his tutors was once heard to growl. I was up with him you see, which makes me—but I won't dwell too much on that. Let's just say that like the king in the play, I'm the oldest man I know.

I suppose I was a pal of his, as much as anybody could really claim to be a pal of Col's. The attraction of opposites, or

* See my story 'Synth'—KR.

something of the sort; me scratching along on a grant and fumbling for a pass via history and Eng. Lit., Col with Eton behind him and money still to burn, cutting every lecture in sight and still managing to come up smelling violets. He'd always buck me up though, if I got too low; tell me there was a lot I could do that he couldn't get near. 'The humanities,' he said to me once, 'never were my long suit, old chap.' Just how true that was, I was one day to find out.

I think there must have been times when we were both written off as lost causes. In my case it damned near turned out to be right, till I had a last minute rush of blood and got my scrape pass after all. Col, of course, picked up a double First, after which our paths rapidly diverged. I went on to—but it doesn't really matter what I went on to do. I made a living, for which I'm grateful; I also stagnated, while Col's star continued its hectic rise. Anybody who'd taken him for a layabout with more money than sense was rapidly disabused; he got his first Chair in a time most folk simply dismissed as indecent, but that was only the start. The letters after his name soon stretched half down an average-sized title page; a fact I had plenty of opportunity to observe, as he was producing books at the rate of anything up to half a dozen a year. Which I realize might not be considered much of a trick in some circles; the thing was though that most of his trifles wound up being definitive. The subjects amazed too. Electronics, engineering, biochemistry, cybernetics; name a discipline, and it seemed he was its master. He could explain it as well, in a way that left even a sentimental duffer like me not gasping too hard for breath. By that time he was already what they used to call a TV personality; what between that, his lecture tours and some score or so of directorships, people wondered how he fitted it all into a working day. Part of the answer, certainly, was an eidetic memory; show him a book page for ten seconds and months later he'd reel off the text, to the last full stop. There was far more to it than that though. I've heard it claimed that the average human being has the equivalent of twenty million volumes of information stored in his head. Doctor Colin Lowston was very far from average; and he could access the whole library.

We kept vaguely in touch for a few years; cards at Christmas, reunion dinners, that sort of thing. I remember he even sent down copies of the first few of what he was pleased to call his scribblings. After which, between his globetrotting and certain involvements of my own, we simply lost touch; for good, as I thought at the time. I wonder now if it would have been better if I'd been right; but that's a story I'll come to in a minute. I still continued to snap his stuff up though, as fast as it came into print. As I said, he was a past master of exposition; but there was something else. When Col put up a proposition, however outlandish and wild, then somehow you believed it. Some of his flights of fancy certainly seemed crazy at the time, though one by one I've watched them all come true. Not least of them of course are the Synths.

He first mooted the idea in one of those innumerable books. *Note on a New Humanity*, it was called; I've still got a copy of it on my shelf. First edition too; it must be worth a few decacredits by now. Not that I'd part with it. It's been with me now just that bit too long.

At first sight I thought he'd gone political; but I needn't have bothered. Col was born where the politicians of this world leave off. What he posited instead was something so outlandish I wondered if he'd finally flipped his lid. One day, he claimed, there'd be a race of androids—or Synthetics, as he styled them—so biologically accurate the only way we'd tell them from ourselves would be by their perfection; a perfection not only of the body, but of the mind. He then proceeded to demolish every argument that could conceivably be ranged against his bright new toy. Metal and plastic prostheses had already replaced most joints of the human body; and had proved themselves far more durable than mere bone. A baby's hands, if made of high grade steel, would wear to the wrists by the age of five; he'd done some calculations himself, and reckoned the estimate to be on the optimistic side. What he proposed instead was a self-renewing, carbon based polymer; in a word, flesh. How such a substance could be brought into being was wholly beyond me of course, and for once he didn't trouble to explain; though knowing Colin he had more than the glimmerings of an idea. As for energy requirements; planes had already flown by the power of the sun itself, drawn themselves into the sky like so many drops of dew.

I remember pulling a bit of a face at that. Poetry, after all, was supposed to be my department.

The media of the time took the matter up with their customary enthusiasm; anything Colin Lowston said was deemed to be news. I watched the first interview he gave. He'd changed a bit since the days I'd known him. His hair, always thin, had greyed prematurely, and retreated to an appropriate professorial fringe; but the old Col was still very much in evidence. There was the same Puckish lift to the eyebrows, the same calculated casualness, the same bantering delivery, half deprecatory, half mocking. As I said, he *gave* the interview; and that was typical too. There was always an air about him, whoever he was with and whatever he was doing, that there was something somewhere else that was really more deserving of his attention. Maybe in his case it was true; or maybe I'm simply describing the Oxbridge of the last few hundred years.

The interviewer, obviously forearmed, tried something of the same approach; but he was wasting his time, he was dealing with another pro. 'Tell me, Doctor Lowston,' he said tolerantly, 'are you asking us to *believe* in these . . . ah . . . figurines of yours?'

Colin considered. 'On the whole, I don't think I am,' he said brightly. 'I've placed certain possibilities before you. Whether you accept them . . . that's rather up to you, isn't it? Hardly my department any more . . .'

'I notice that in your book you skirt round the problem of intelligence.'

'Do I, indeed?' said Col, unperturbed. 'Good Lord, I hadn't realized.' He clasped his hands under his chin. 'I suppose one *could* read pages one four two to one eight three; but this is a video age . . . Have you come across Hubert Wolfenden?'

'*The* Hubert Wolfenden? British Computers?'

'The same. Used to be a colleague of mine. Well, Hubert's got a rather pretty idea. Sort of a semiconducting matrix. Like cotton wool. Or candyfloss. Chop it up by the yard; with garden shears, if necessary. One rather envisages . . . ah . . . stuffing it into the cranium.' He looked thoughtful. 'Connections to the motor centres could be a bit of a problem; but I think we can get round that.'

The interviewer's look said a lot. 'I was given to understand that brain tissue was somewhat more delicate.'

'Oh, no, no, no, no, no,' said Colin cheerfully. 'Dear me, no. Doesn't seem to be really all that important, as a matter of fact. There was that chappie in the States, blew a crowbar through his head. Lived to a ripe old age. And there are quite a few hydrocephalous subjects with Degrees. For what that's worth.' He looked apologetic. 'Point taken. You're probably right after all . . .'

His would-be tormentor wouldn't relinquish the bone. 'I take it then you'll be sidestepping microchip technology.'

'And why not?' said Col blandly. 'Ninety per cent of the bloody things are rejects anyway. Manufacturing faults. Rather inefficient, wouldn't you say?'

Then of course the inevitable business about library volumes came up. But he brushed that aside as well. 'I'd say twenty million books was aiming a trifle high. Wouldn't need 'em, of course. I'd start with a couple of sections; say about a hundred thousand. Got to leave room for the dry cells, after all.'

'Dry cells?'

Colin smiled. 'In case the sun goes in . . .'

The interviewer sighed. 'Doctor Lowston, if we could move on . . . what . . . er . . . sex would these creatures be?'

Colin wrinkled his forehead. 'Now that *is* a tricky one. Too many choices, really . . .'

'I would have thought,' said the other tartly, 'that there were only two . . .'

Colin beamed at him. 'Ah, there you go,' he said happily. 'The good old blinkered thinking, where would we be without it? There's probably two hundred. Or two thousand. As many as you want. Don't forget we're not talking biologically.'

The interviewer set his lips. 'Very well. Avoiding then what seems to be a delicate area—'

'Not delicate at all,' said Colin chirpily. He slapped a thin folder that lay on the table in front of him 'Had some market research people look into it. They suggest, initially at least, ah . . . female. Considering the current state of chauvinism, I rather suspect they're right. Can't rush our fences, you know. Got to consider the consumer . . .'

The interviewer shut the notes he carried with a snap. 'Well, Doctor, I must say you sound most convincing. But for the sake of us mere mortals, can you give me any idea what these creatures of yours would look like?'

'The Creatures of Prometheus,' said Colin musingly. 'Hardly flattering . . . but yes, I think I can.' He swung a keyboard in front of him, tapped out a code; and a monitor screen at his elbow lit up. The studio camera zoomed in on it, and cut.

I'd seen computer graphics often enough before; and fairly unconvincing most of them had looked. The craft was after all still in its infancy; now it seemed that infancy was over. The face that appeared seemed to build itself up from a skull; but that process was too lightning-fast to follow. The jawline firmed and steadied; the hair arranged itself, bunching round a narrow, embroidered fillet; finally and dramatically, the eyes opened. They were dark and lustrous, magnetic.

'A long-lost glory,' said Colin dreamily. 'Perhaps the Nike of Samothrace. But a little Classical perhaps, for modern taste. Anyway, that sort of thing's all been done . . .'

The skin tones were altering already, deepening and richening to purest ebony. The zygomas broadened, adjusted; the hair plaited itself into a complex, jet coiffure. It hung in pigtails now, each bound with gold, each furbished with a vivid coral bead. She was exquisite; but she was melting again.

'Spoiled for choice, you see,' said the voice-over. 'We thought for a time . . . the Eurasian . . . ideal of female beauty, don't you know. But then, there's so very much . . .'

She was an Aboriginal now; a Brahmin, with skin the colour of palest coffee; an Egyptian girl from high antiquity, her eyelids dark with kohl. And still the skull planes changing, twinkling, modelling the flesh. 'Till finally,' said Colin, 'we thought . . . this is Mark Twenty Three. Or it may even be Twenty Four . . .'

I stared at the screen. The face that watched back seemed somehow blended of all that had gone before. It was, I suppose, that of a white-skinned woman; yet the overall impression was of bronze. Bronze of tanned skin, of eyes, bronze of her straight, lustrous hair. She too wore a fillet, as if she had dressed for some energetic activity; and she, alone of all of them, smiled, turned her head from side to side to show a profile Classic as the first.

Then she was gone, and Col was leaning back in his chair, fingers steepled, nodding as pleasantly, as tolerantly, as before.

There was more to the interview; but I took very little of it in. I was curiously preoccupied by that final image I had seen; the image of something that didn't exist, in heaven or earth. It was a face to challenge the mind, as the faces of dream-folk sometimes do. I was to see it again though, finally; then, it belonged to a personage called Dearbhla Cagnac.

Oddly enough, that was almost Colin's last appearance on what we used to call the Box; at least for many years. It was as if, quite suddenly, he had become bored with the medium, as he so frequently tired of people. Then, for no apparent reason, he'd simply turn on his heel and stalk away; I'd seen him do it often enough in the past. I've come to wonder since whether he didn't merely suck them dry, discard them when they were no further use to him. But maybe that's uncharitable; the general waspishness of age.

As far as I recall, he only graced the little screen once more; and that, presumably, was something he'd committed himself to and couldn't wriggle out of. He looked sullen and bad-tempered, and was brusque with the interviewer—a well-informed and unusually attractive young woman—to the point of rudeness. There'd been a lot of comment in the press, mainly to the effect that despite his claims all he'd demonstrated was an ingenious video; when charged with that he merely answered with Zeno's paradox, or rather his own peculiar version of it. If his Synthetic didn't exist, then nothing had gone away when the switch was turned. If nothing had gone away then something must still be there, waiting to be called back to life. When asked why, with his interest in the then-new field of genetic engineering, he wasn't content to let nature take its course, he answered with quite uncharacteristic bluntness that if the custard was ready, only a damned fool would set about growing rhubarb. And that was that. There was some talk in the press that he was setting up a new company, UK Synthetics; but whether in defiance or desperation nobody could quite say. Generally, he dropped from sight; and the public, lacking further stimulus, turned its gnat-span attention to other more pressing matters. Doctor Lowston and his affairs were forgotten, even by me.

I suppose my reasons were sound enough. The next few years were the brightest time of my life; they were followed by the darkest. I won't go into detail, because it wouldn't interest you; after so long, it doesn't even interest me. Suffice to say that the business I set up thrived beyond my expectations; and that there was a woman. The only one ever, for me. Looking back, it seems the days were always sunny; and we were very much in love. It wasn't always sunny of course; sometimes it rained stair rods, and we fought like cat and dog. That was when she'd swear she'd clear off, leave me to stew. One day I let her, and there was no going back. There's never any going back of course. Afterwards; well, it's a common enough tale, and boring to a degree. Except maybe for those who live it. I started keeping the odd bottle about the place; never felt too happy without one in the house. First it was a nip or two to help me sleep, shut the wind noise out on winter nights. The rest grew from that. There was an old boy round about that time who used to say that drink was the Devil in solution. I'm inclined to believe, after thinking about it a good many years, that he was right.

They wheeled me off finally to dry me out. That took a year or two as well. I'd get myself sorted, go back, start trying to pick up the threads; but there were the old surroundings, the old memories, the cupboard where the whisky used to live. I'd hold out for months sometimes; then the slide would start again. And back I'd go, to the State Home for the Bewildered.

The last jaunt very nearly did for me. Leastways they told me later the prognosis was close enough to zero to make no odds. I thought so as well. Whether that knocked some sense into me at last, or whether I'd finally managed to sicken myself of the whole damned thing, I just couldn't say. But I know a morning came when I stood on the pavement of a little West Country town, and smelled the breeze from the sea, and knew I was going to have to get away; from the town, from the region, from a place I could no longer bear. I got on a train the same afternoon, and finished up in London. Why I headed there I still don't know, except that I needed people round me, streets; somewhere where there were no more distant hills.

Thanks to the kindly laws protecting madmen, I'd still got the remnant at least of what I'd built up. I sold out, lock, stock and barrel, sat down to count what was left. It wasn't a fortune by any stretch, but with care I reckoned it might see me through. I rented a flatlet off what used to be the Portobello Road, moved in some sticks of furniture and my books and settled down to while away my middle age. I suppose you'll think that was a queer sort of existence to choose; but then, I'd done all the high living I was interested in. For one incarnation at least.

Later I even got myself a little job, wheeling clapped-out antiques from one end of the Market to the other; and back again of course, ready for the next day's punters. It gave me a bit of beer money—shorts strictly out—and there was even the odd perk thrown in. I picked up a battered trivee rig for next to nothing, got it installed. I couldn't have run to a hologram receiver even if I'd wanted to, but the old set served; it helped to break the evenings up as well.

One of the first things I noticed was that Col Lowston was back on the scene; and not looking a day older, blast him. To my surprise, he was heavily into sport; though of course he brought his own unique approach to everything he touched. He'd designed a radically new type of golf club, with some sort of fancy shaft that he reckoned would increase a top class player's drive by up to twenty per cent; the various interested bodies were currently conferring about whether they'd allow the things to be used in the international circuit at all. Rumour had it that he'd spent a fortune on a racing yacht—designed by him, of course—that would finally bring the America's Cup back to Britain, while he was currently turning his attention to the humble cricket bat, with results that promised to be equally dire. I didn't know quite what to make of it. At College he'd always reserved his sharpest gibes for the flannelled fools at the wicket. I finally decided he'd made his stack, and opted for resting on his laurels; I only hoped they smelled a bit sweeter than mine.

I'd developed quite an interest in sport myself, in a strictly voyeuristic way. Still, the old trivee served me well enough. I'd always been a bit of a cricket buff; but to that the media magnates, in their endless search for novelty—and with six whole channels to fill—had added everything from Pall-Mall to Jai Alai. Even the wild, brilliant game of hurling was enjoying a

UK vogue; it jockeyed for airtime with more conventional pursuits like baseball and golf. It took me awhile to get round to watching tennis again though; rather too many painful memories.

I was drawn in, finally, by the great annual tournament at Wimbledon. I say 'drawn in' deliberately, because the process was accompanied by a certain sturdy resistance. I was long past the hero-worship stage; I knew it for a hard, rich, cutthroat game, and entertained more than a suspicion that the glittering personages who played the international circuit were in it, first and foremost, for the cash. Leastways if they didn't make it while they could they were bigger fools than I thought; and they didn't look like fools at all to me. But there was always an aura about Wimbledon, a special magic to which I finally succumbed.

Maybe I should explain. In those days, cricket and tennis were played on stuff called grass. No blue and yellow mats, no ads, no blasts of organ music; just the wind in folks' hair, and the sun. I know there's a Wimbledon Centre now of course, there's still a tournament; but the place I'm speaking of wasn't a highrise tower. There were creeper-hung balconies, a great jigsaw puzzle of courts; the clouds sailed over and the birds, on good days you even saw the odd butterfly. And that, I suppose, was the charm. Locked away as I was, and as I intended to remain, it was my private breath of summer, faithfully renewed.

As I began to follow the game its personalities, all new since my day, grew into sharper relief. Chris Walewski, everybody's pet hate, who'd carved her way through the ratings, as far as I could see, by a combination of skill, brute force and plain intimidation; Anna Schroeder, my ideal American, elegant and gentle, two Wimbledons under her belt and looking for a third; Cirri Pütsjarvi, the compact, cheerful little lass they called the Flying Finn; and many more. By which you'll gather I rather favoured the ladies. That may seem curious, and very probably is. I can only—and as Col Lowton once remarked, your belief isn't my concern—that I was neither an old fool nor a dirty one. As a lad, I'd been a confirmed balletomane. The music, settings, decor, might not have meant too much; but the line of a great ballerina was a ravishment to the eye. In these top players of all—excluding the fearsome Walewski, who was an exception to every rule—I saw that line again. Aestheticism, you see, can occasionally remain, even when all the rest has been leached away.

It was a year or so later that Sarah Foster first entered the international lists. From the first, as far as the media were concerned, she was the Girl from Dorset; and from the first I was electrified. The long-tailed, sea blue eyes, the fair hair she drew up like the tail of a pony or horse, her pert, lissome figure, created emotions in me I find hard to describe; while the nation, of course, took her to its heart at once. Here was a girl, it was said, who for the first time in a generation stood a real chance of making it to the top; at long, long last, Britain would have a First again. Nor, proclaimed the media, was she remotely like the rest; she was someone to whom reward was secondary, someone who truly lived for her sport. For once, I was inclined to believe the ballyhoo. She had about her a curious vulnerability; tomboyish in victory, jaded in defeat. Sometimes, bite her lip as she might, the tears would well; the camera caught them of course, every time. In interview she was modest, almost shy; quick to praise her opponents, always ready to deprecate herself. She was, in a word, enchanting; and absurd though it will undoubtedly seem, my worry for her steadily grew. The hopes of too many folk were resting on her; those shoulders, at times, seemed far too slim for the load.

Somewhere in the world, there was a major tournament at least once a week; with the new satellites beaming programmes down round the clock, there was tennis to be seen at all hours of the day and night. She seemed to be everywhere as well; so much so that I determined that somehow or other I had to have a triVCR. There Ronnie, the guy I worked for, came up trumps. He was good to me over the cassettes too. Which lorry they were falling off I never enquired; nor did I care. The recordings filled two shelves, began to jostle my books aside. Sarah in Athens, Sarah in New York; Sarah in Rome, Sarah in Milan. If grit and determination counted for anything, she seemed well on the way to fulfilling the prophecies made for her. She rose swiftly in the computer's good books; after a year she rated twelfth in the world, after eighteen months an incredible seventh. It was at that point that I wrote to her. Why, I'm unable to say; I'd never done such a thing before, and I'm not likely now to do it again. I hardly expected an answer. Nonetheless one came; on pale beige paper, with a big cuddly panda at the top and the motto SAVE THE ANIMALS. There were few animals left by that time of course, apart from us; what it really should have said was 'Save the Zoos'. It didn't matter though; I was still entranced. I found a frame for it, hung it in pride of place above the mantel. Ronnie, dropping in for the odd beer, looked at it more than once and pursed his lips, but made no comment. That didn't worry me either; he could think what he liked. The envelope, with its exotic foreign stamp, I tucked carefully away; because her hand had touched it.

Then the bad luck began. First it was a car smash, that left her in plaster for weeks. For some time there was doubt that she'd ever walk properly again, let alone play tennis. How I felt is best left to the imagination. Suffice to say that if I could have got my hands round the neck of the fool who was driving I'd have committed murder without a qualm.

Not only did she play again, she won the Paris Open that very year; though what the comeback cost her, only she will ever know. It seemed she was on course again; but the respite was brief. A whole series of minor problems kept her from tournament after tournament; after which she seemed totally to have lost her form. Nothing went right for her; the old bounce and sparkle simply weren't there and her rating, that had already fallen disastrously, slumped yet again. Naturally, the rumours started. Her name was linked with this and that jetsetter; all of which I discounted till news came through of a whirlwind courtship, marriage with a New York tycoon who must have been twenty years her senior. I groaned aloud, not believing my ears. She'd sold out it seemed; for a mansion in Pennsylvania, a yacht, a stable of fast cars. I realize now of course that I was wrong; because six months later the marriage was in ruins. She sold herself defiantly to the American circuit; but that didn't last long either. Before the year was up she'd bought out of her contract and come home, reputedly for good. It didn't stop the whispering though. She'd retired altogether from tennis; she'd borne a secret child; she'd taken up with the Hari Krishna sect. Finally she dropped from sight completely, and the word went out that she had gone to India to study with a guru. True or no, somewhere she found the inner strength she'd searched for so desperately; because she reappeared at Eastbourne, stormed through the opposition like the champion we all knew she could be. Next stop was Wimbledon.

A few days later I bumped into Colin Lowston. Almost literally. I was manoeuvring a bulky chest of drawers through the doorway of the shop; the whole thing tilted, and I thought for a moment we were going to be in for some hefty damages. He steadied it in the nick of time; I said 'Thanks' automatically, then looked up. I said, 'Good Lord . . .'

He was grinning his broadest grin. 'How are you, you old bugger?' he said, 'How are you?' He grabbed my hand. 'Must have been centuries . . .'

I'd thought for an odd second that he wouldn't be pleased to see me after so many years, that he'd make some excuse and hurry on his way. It would after all have been far from untypical. Not a bit of it though. 'What've you been doing with yourself?' he said. 'Where's your pad? I've got an hour or two to kill; mind if we have a yak?'

It was nearly knocking off time anyway; I indicated the flat, and nothing would suffice but that he hare off to the old corner shop. He was back in minutes with his arms full of goodies; French loaves and paté, a generous hunk of cheese, a couple of bottles of plonk. 'Bloody ravenous,' he said. 'Haven't eaten all day. Tend to lose track of time; sign of age, y'know. I say, this is cosy. Wouldn't mind it m'self . . .'

I spread a tablecloth; admittedly a somewhat rare event. 'What are you doing in town anyway?' I said. 'Last place I'd expect to see you.'

'Oh, this and that,' he said vaguely. 'Browsing. Never could resist junkshops; still looking for that undiscovered Raphael.'

I let the crack about the junkshops pass. It was ninety per cent true anyway. I opened the wine instead, poured a couple of glasses. I said, 'It's good to see you, Colin,' and he beamed again. 'Me too,' he said. 'It's good to see *you*.' For once, he sounded almost as if he meant it.

We sat and nattered, in fact, far longer than two hours. I told him, briefly, what had happened to me, the cockup I'd made of my life. He listened, lips pursed and nodding, but made no comment. Instead he sketched in some of the things he'd been getting up to in the past few years; and pretty amazing stuff it was, though I've no room to set it down here. After which I boiled up some coffee, hunted out a couple of cigars. We sat and reminisced about old times in general till suddenly he looked down at his wrist. 'Have to break it up I'm afraid, old chap,' he said. 'Early start tomorrow, long day . . .'

'Can I get you a cab?' I said. 'It's not the best area for walking after dark, you know.'

'Wouldn't hear of it,' he said cheerfully. 'Rank just round the corner, be there in a jiff.' He skipped through the front door; but halfway down the steps he turned. 'I say, do you plan on watching Wimbledon?'

'Try and keep me away,' I said. 'I take half days off for the fortnight. Why?'

He grinned. 'Good. should be rather interesting this year. Main reason I've come up, in fact. Well, cheerio; and I'll be in touch. Mustn't let another quarter century slip by . . .'

I closed the door, thoughtfully. I was wondering what the devil he could have meant. One fact was certain; there was something behind it. Because I'd never yet known him say a thing without a reason.

The Wimbledon of that year promised to be the best on record. There were the usual gripes about the seedings and the price of strawberries, the usual gloomy prognostications as to the weather; but that's all part of the fun of the thing, and expected. Not unnaturally though, the chief topic of conversation among the pundits was Miss Sarah Foster. Had she found her form at last? And could she, this time, keep her game together? How would she fare against Chris Walewski, to whom she'd lost decisively on their last half dozen meetings? Always assuming, of course, she stayed alive that long. Nobody, I noticed, pondered the outcome of a match between her and the great Anna Schroeder, now in contention for her fifth singles title; by which I assumed the general consensus was that she wouldn't.

In the event the tournament opened under skies of burning blue, a state of affairs the forecasters assured us cheerfully would last throughout the fortnight. Din Mahommed, reigning men's champion, defended his title with customary vigour; Anna, in her mandatory opening match, gave a classically cool display against a little Netherlander who seemed too overawed by the occasion to put up much resistance. The lobs fell with merciless accuracy, each within inches of the line; and I found myself shaking my head. I too, were I to be honest with myself, gave Sarah little chance.

However she survived, battling on gamely in her own section, though not without a few heartstopping moments. The crowds, of course, were with her to a man, or woman; for my part, stupid though it will undoubtedly sound, I sat for much of the time with her framed letter on my knee, pressing my palm to the glass as if I could somehow transmit a strength to her. Maybe it helped, I wouldn't know; I'm sure Col Lowston would say stranger things have happened.

The tournament proceeded smoothly enough till the end of the first week, which found Walewski giving a particularly vitriolic display for the benefit of a game young American. As usual, she had brought a small but vociferous band of supporters with her; the cushions were raining down, and the scorer booming about penalty points, when the commentator broke in excitedly. 'And now we're leaving this for a moment and going over to Number Twelve Court, where I'm told something truly remarkable is happening . . .'

The image flickered and changed. For a moment it seemed they had trouble with the cameras, out in that distant precinct. Then the picture brightened; the tiny figures steadied, below me on the grass. The scoreboard told its own story; love six, love four. The server was Cirri Pütsjarvi.

Her first ball was a good one, fast and deep. It was answered, extraordinarily, by a wicked slice that curled away over the net, leaving her no chance. So were the second and third. The fourth she got her racquet to, in a desperate attempt to lob, but to no avail; Out was called, leaving her opponent serving for the match. Her first ball aced the Finn, streaking down the centreline to rebound from the screening with a wicked thump. The canvas shook from side to side, and I blinked. Never could I remember seeing a ball hit as hard as that; and certainly not by a woman. The second Cirri returned, by the merest reflex action. It flew high and wide, and would almost certainly have gone out; but her opponent, already at the net, despatched it anyway with a viperish crosscourt volley. Two more unplayable aces followed, and it was all over. 'And so,' babbled the commentator, 'the number three seed goes out; in love sets, to a complete unknown. Well, what a turnup; what a turnup for the book . . .'

I wasn't listening. My back felt icy, and the room was evincing a strong tendency to rotate. For the cameras had zoomed in, first to show Cirri's stricken face, then to focus on the stranger. She turned, smiling, reached up formally to touch the referee's hand. For a moment, it seemed her eyes looked straight into mine; and in that second I knew her. Hers was a face I hadn't seen for more years than I cared to remember; but equally it was one I could never forget. Because the last time it had stared at me, it was from the heart of a computer.

She was grabbed for interview of course within minutes; it was no surprise to see Col Lowston with her, fussing about like a mother hen. It was only then I fully realized what a striking woman she was; tall and graceful, with delicately modelled legs. No hint of that stringiness that sometimes afflicts even the best of women athletes. She had poise too, and a rare elegance; not a hair out of place, and as composed as if she'd just come in from a gentle stroll, rather than off that burning-hot court. I put her age at twenty one or two; but with that face, it was almost impossible. She could have been—but Heaven knows, really, what she could have been.

The interviewer riffled a sheaf of papers. 'Tell me Miss Cagnac, your . . . er . . . first name. How do you . . .'

'The aitch mutes the consonant before it,' she said, smiling. 'Just as in English.'

He looked, if possible, more unsure than ever. 'Well, er . . . yes. Miss Cagnac, that was a truly remarkable performance, truly remarkable. And of course, a quarter final qualifier; which means you'll be meeting . . .'

'Walewski, without a doubt,' said Col. He seemed to be relishing the situation.

'Er . . . yes,' said the interviewer. 'Yes, it's coming through on this funny little earpiece thing . . . Yes, she's through. So that really should be quite a match . . .'

Miss Cagnac inclined her head, graciously.

'Tell me—I'm not going to try that first name, I'm bound to get it wrong—tell me, how were you able to lift your play so radically? I mean, you've played extremely well to get so far; but this . . .' He seemed genuinely at a loss for words.

The other raised her chin. 'Miss Pütsjarvi is a very fine performer,' she said. 'I have great respect for her. One must always do one's best to win.' She fixed him with her disturbing eyes; and he turned to Colin, it seemed in self defence. 'Doctor Lowston, I understand Miss Cagnac is your protégé?'

'Very much so,' said Colin, and grinned again. Everything, it seemed, was all right with his world.

'But who trained her? Where . . .'

'I did, I suppose,' said Col. 'Well, it was more of a team effort really . . .'

The girl turned to give his wrist a little squeeze. 'Whatever I am, I owe to him,' she said. 'He is always far too modest.'

I frowned. Her voice was soft, with a hint of huskiness; but there was something in the intonation that I just couldn't place. Her first name, certainly, was Irish, her surname almost had a Breton ring; the accent belonged to neither. I decided I'd simply never heard it before.

Colin stood up, briskly. 'Well, I'm afraid Dearbhla must rest now, she's had a busy day. So if you'll excuse us, I'm sure you understand . . .'

'Thank you,' said the interviewer. 'Thank you, Miss Cagnac. And . . . er . . . good luck with the quarter finals . . .'

Cirri was more forthright. '*Wow*, it come,' she said. 'Straight down the middle line. Think for a minute it knock ruddy hole in me. Wow . . .' She stuck her lip out, blew upwards at her fringe and rolled her eyes. 'And she not even sweating . . .' Then, typically, she grinned. 'Good luck anyway,' she said. 'She player, never seen like her before . . .'

In its own way it was a small enough remark; but it was enough to set the press baying on the scent. Most of the Monday papers carried screaming headlines WIMBLEDON MYSTERY: THE GIRL WHO CAN'T PERSPIRE. *Is She What She Seems?* It was obvious some valiant digging had been going on; somebody had even unearthed a tape of Colin's old programme, though the studio videos themselves had not been retained. So I was never able to prove, to anybody else at least, what I had seen.

Colin himself was unavailable for comment. He had stolen a march on his pursuers; sometime during the evening following the match a helicopter landed on the roof pad of his hotel, whisked him and the girl off to an unknown destination. They had been accompanied, according to a reporter blessed either with unusually keen sight or an abnormally powerful imagination, by 'half a dozen white-coated men, very obviously lab technicians.' I guessed at some hand-wringing behind the urbane face of the All England Club; for the match was scheduled for two in the afternoon.

The arrival was made in style, the chopper swooping down to the accompaniment of cheers from the crowds that packed the approaches for a quarter mile around. From it, as *chic* and unruffled as ever, stepped the enigmatic Miss Cagnac, Colin bobbing delightedly at her side. Mounted police surged forward; others, hatless and sweating, linked their arms, leaned back on the crowds to force a passage to the ground. Newsmen scurried with their microphones and cameras; but all were disappointed. The gates banged shut, the fists of the mob resumed their rhythmic, muffled beating.

It had been timed to a hair. Dearbhla stepped onto Court Number Two, where Walewski already stood scowling and tapping her foot, at exactly five to the hour. The toss was made, the knockup proceeded; 'Two minutes, ladies,' was called, and the protégée slipped off the light jacket she had worn. She was dressed as before in brilliant white, the stitching of the fillet round her brow the only spark of colour. Play was ordered, Miss Walewski to serve; and a total hush descended.

It didn't last long; Chris had obviously decided a counter demonstration was in order. Her first return, which seemed to me a good six inches out, was duly called as such; and a familiar squalling rose. The umpire, summoned from his haven of retreat, confirmed both line judge and referee; but Walewski was barely into her stride.

At love forty, after penalties for abuse of the racquet and audible obscenity, she condescended to play on. Dearbhla, who had kept her back squarely to the fracas, turned to face the court; a delicate lob raised chalk dust from the baseline, and it was first game to Miss Cagnac.

I watched as puzzled as the rest. There was none of the pulverising strength I'd seen a day or so before; instead the gentle, accurate ground shots went on and on. Time after time the tall girl opened the court, sending her opponent skidding desperately from side to side, but the smash that should have killed the ball just never came; time after time, it was returned quietly into play. The unforced errors mounted, till belatedly the answer came. She was Walewski's measure; and she was toying with her.

I think the notion dawned on the Polish girl at one and the same time. Her eyes contracted with fury; but it was too late, she was already on the run. She turned and leaped, performing prodigies, contacting ball after ball that miraculously seemed to pitch just within her reach. Dark vees of sweat grew on her chest and back; the microphones picked up her gasps for breath, mixed with the hard, erratic thudding of the racquets.

I don't know whether you've ever heard a tendon snap. I have, just once, and wouldn't particularly want to again. It seemed the sound echoed across the court like a pistol shot; it was followed by a thin, high scream of agony. Then Walewski was rolling on the ground, clutching her leg, while Dearbhla sauntered to the chair to demand the point. 'The noise she made distracted me,' she said coolly.

I couldn't believe my eyes. The Pole shoved away the officials who ran to her, got to her feet and staggered to the baseline. How she stood at all I couldn't imagine; it was raw courage, and nothing else, that kept her going. Her opponent shaped to serve; and over floated the sort of lob you'd see in a Sunday park. So the dreadful game of pat-a-cake was to be prolonged.

The crowd was on its feet. I think I was probably shouting too. Over the years, she'd taken every mean advantage. She'd been the scourge of ball boys, linesmen, referees and players alike; in my eyes she'd brought a great event into disorder and disrepute. But she hadn't deserved what was being done to her; nobody deserved that. The loudspeakers were booming for quiet; but the game went on regardless. Because one player couldn't hear the din, and the other didn't care.

A quick shot showed Col Lowston sitting back, expressionless; beside him Sarah was hiding her face. Dearbhla glanced across; and whether some signal passed between them I couldn't say. But her shoulders came back at last; and over went the crashing aces that ended the whole sorry affair. The speakers pealed, faint in the din, for game, set and match; and Chris Walewski, blood on her chin, dropped to her knees, bowed her forehead to the grass. I stamped across the room, slapped at the stop button of the VCR and set it to erase.

Anna Schroeder's turn came just forty eight hours later. Naturally there had been immense speculation about just what tactics the newcomer would employ against the great baseliner, but nobody second-guessed the event itself; she baselined. Anna tried everything she knew; drop shots and stopped volleys, ground strokes that dipped and swung like birds in flight, the flashing backhand pass that many reckoned to be virtually unplayable. The rallies stretched endlessly, forty, fifty strokes at a time; but always, finally, it was the American who was drawn to the net. Then, with mathematical precision, would come the lob; and each and every ball raised its puff of dust from the line. As the score inexorably mounted, the crowd fell curiously quiet; till finally Anna's clear, brittle little 'Yep' announced before the speakers that the match was over.

An odd thing happened then. As if on impulse Dearbhla dropped her racquet, raced round the net into her opponent's court. The other flung her hair back, wiped tiredly at her eyes; and the tall girl gripped her shoulders, in a gesture of sympathy. I may be crazy, and very probably am, but it seemed to me that what was conveyed above all else was the notion of regret for the thing she had been called on to do. The photographers ran forward, intent to catch the moment; and just before the applause started a solitary voice spoke somewhere. Some fluke of acoustics carried it to the microphones; it said, '*Reprogrammed . . .*'

In the rush of extraordinary events my little Sarah had been, it seemed, all but forgotten. It was not the case though; the audience measurement folk claimed later that more people watched the second semi-final than any other match in the tournament. Nell Patterson, the Australian allrounder, had been slowed by a torn groin muscle; but the battle was still a dour one, the hardest, probably, of the English girl's career. I watched it with feelings about as mixed as they could be. On the one hand stood the glittering prize toward which Sarah's whole life had been aimed; but on the other stood Dearbhla and the man I was coming to think of, slowly but surely, as her master. What they might hatch between them I had no idea; but the thought of it struck with a sudden chill.

Colin rang me a few minutes after the transmission ended. He sounded very much his old, chirpy self. 'Well,' he said, 'coming along on Friday to see Sarah win her pot? I've got a couple of spare tickets; we can do it in style.'

I'd forgotten of course that he was a Member as well; but then, he was a member of almost everything. 'No thanks,' I said slowly, 'I don't think I will.'

The phone clucked at me. 'Don't be an ass old man, bloody things are like gold dust. Why ever not?'

I said, 'I think you know why not. Anyway, she doesn't stand a chance.'

He considered. 'Never lost until it's won, you know,' he said. 'Or something like that. In any case, she'll need all the support she can get.'

I hesitated. Somehow to be near her, physically near, for the first time in my life; the thought had a certain giddying appeal. To be on hand, in case of—what? There was nothing I could do to influence affairs, one way or the other. 'I'd never make it,' I said. 'Not if the crowds are anything like the other day.'

''Course you will,' he said briskly. 'I'll send a car round for you. Better make it nineish, before things warm up too much; give us a chance for the odd pre-prandial too.'

I hesitated again. 'Look, Colin,' I said, 'just one thing. I don't know what your game is, but if anything happens to that kid . . . Watch yourself, won't you? Because I'll not be answerable . . .'

He chuckled. 'I've told you what's going to happen,' he said. 'See you in the morning.' There was a click, and the buzz of a disconnected line.

I'd never been inside the Centre Court before. Somehow the place seemed at the same time both more intimate and more massive than I had envisaged. Trivee, for all its good points, gave you some funny notions of proportion and perspective.

What it could never have conveyed though, not in a million years, was the sheer electric tension of the place; an almost tangible buzz that set the adrenalin to flowing, the heart to pumping just that fraction faster than normal. I was regretting now the sour view I'd once taken of the players. I was a mere spectator; what I was feeling was a shadow of what they must go through, down there on the worn oblong of grass.

I looked across to the scoreboard, peered past the stand roof at the brilliant wedge of sky. Puffy white clouds were chasing themselves across my angle of vision. A bird swooped, sudden, and was gone; I was reminded for some reason of the acres of empty courts surrounding us. The whole great festival had closed in on itself, focused for this one day on a nucleus. Then Colin touched my arm.

She was tinier than I'd imagined; daintier, and infinitely more pretty. Applause for her thundered, filling the high space round me; I heard it dimly, as if coming from a distance. My attention was wholly engaged; with textures of hair and skin, brilliant line of the skirt across her thigh, her hands as they fiddled with the ribbon in her hair, adjusted a sock, a shoelace. Again, I was well served out; it was no more than I deserved though, for trying to live with my head inside a box. I was stunned by what must appear a simple, banal truth; that she, that all of this, was *real*.

I couldn't remember the last time I'd driven a car; it was hard to believe just how rusty I'd got. The roads too, with their over-passes, underpasses and multiple lanes, just weren't the roads I remembered. It was a relief when the gates of the estate finally swung into sight. I turned in past the lodges, drove till I could see the house. And some house it was too, new, low wings stretching out on either side of the Tudor frontage. Above were the great stacks with their twisted, latticed pots. A fountain played, centrepiece of an immaculate lawn; beyond was the first of the superb, jewel-green courts. I saw the net was strung, as if a match was imminent.

Quite why I'd taken up Colin's invitation I couldn't say; except that somehow or other the affair of Dearbhla Cagnac just had to be resolved. 'Come down,' was all he'd said. 'I think you'll find it interesting . . .' And that was that. I havered for a while; finally I knew there was no way I could ignore it. And so the car was hired; into the tank went the best part of a month's allowance.

It was two days after the fiasco of the Final; six love, six love to Sarah Foster, against a player who moved with the awkwardness and uncertainty of a wooden doll. The crowd, stunned at first, had finally grown restive; and match point was greeted not with the storm it should have caused, but with derisive cheers. The clockwork business of the presentation proceeded; the carpet was rolled out, the ball boys scurried into their lines, Sarah swung the great salver over her head one final time. I wasn't close enough to see her face too clearly; but I could guess at the expression it bore. Victorious she was, in no uncertain terms; but the triumph was hollow. She had been given a bye.

Colin met me at the door, in check shirt and casual slacks. His manner was as breezy as ever. 'Glad you could make it, old chap,' he said. 'Come in, I'll show you round . . .' And show me round he did, through room after room crammed with pictures, antiques, *objets d'art*. I rapidly gave up trying to estimate the value; I hadn't brought a calculator with me.

Last stop was the music room, housed in one of the new wings and presided over by a massive eighteenth-century harpsichord. Aquarium tanks let into the walls displayed a collection of British pond life; interspersed with them were the speakers of a massive multichannel hifi. I stared round vaguely; but I wasn't really registering too well. 'Colin,' I said, 'why did you want me here? What are you setting up now?'

'A meeting,' he said, grinning. 'I thought you might be interested. And here she is too, by Jove; dead on cue.' He nodded toward the glass wall that closed off one side of the place. Between the estate trees a small red car was approaching at high speed.

He met her on the verandah with its leaden statues, its tubs of trailing plants. 'I don't think you've been properly introduced,' he said. 'John Cunningham, a very old friend of mine; Miss Sarah Foster . . .'

But she had scant time for me. 'Where is she,' she said. '*Where is she* . . . ?' She'd even come dressed for tennis, and there were racquets in her arms. 'You promised,' she said. Colin began to speak again; and she yelled at him. 'Will you fetch her? Or shall I find her myself . . .'

'There's no need,' said a quiet voice behind us. 'Good afternoon, Miss Foster . . .'

She stepped out from the house. Up close, she was more spectacular than ever; the golden skin, the golden hair and eyes. She wore shorts, and a casually-knotted sun top. Her feet were bare, a chunky bracelet tinkled at her wrist; over the other arm she carried a woolly. She made to speak; but Sarah cut her off. 'I want to play tennis,' she said. 'And I want *him* to keep away. Him and his bloody little black box . . .'

Colin's grin became broader; he pulled his slacks pockets inside out. 'Never use the things,' he said. 'Had to give 'em up. Doctor's orders . . .'

For a moment, I thought she would attack him. She turned away, swallowed and pointed. 'Come on,' she said.

Dearbhla smiled. 'I'm sorry,' she said, 'but I can't oblige you, Sarah.' She slipped the cardigan from her arm. On her wrist was a neat white bandage. 'I strained it this morning, at practice,' she said. 'I couldn't hold a racquet if I tried.'

There was a silence that went on. Sarah stared from her to Colin, and back. Finally she walked up to her. 'Who are you?' she said. '*What* are you? *Just tell me* . . .'

Dearbhla smiled. 'Someone who gets nerves on Finals day,' she said. 'You ought to know about things like that.'

Colin rubbed his hands. 'Well,' he said, 'It's rather muggy this afternoon. I suggest we all take some tea.'

A table was brought to the verandah, and a tray with mounds of thin-cut bread. A Georgian pot steamed gently; and there were silver bowls heaped with strawberries and cream. Dearbhla sat, gracefully. 'I'll be mother,' she said. She filled the cups, and passed them; she took a slice of bread, bisected it neatly with a knife. She ate it, slowly, her eyes on Sarah's face. Then she picked up a spoon. 'The strawberries are good this year,' she said. 'All home grown too.'

Sarah's chair went over. She ran; and there was the screech of car tyres on gravel. Then the engine sound, revving far too high in first, fading among the trees that lined the drive.

I expect you've all heard car crashes on the trivee; all that tinkling and crumbling, in glamorous overlay. In real life of course they're not like that at all. The single, hollow *bonk* sounded as if a giant had struck a dustbin with a mallet, out there among the trees. Then there was silence; and the birds still sang. Dearbhla jerked round, stared; then she was up, and running. Colin followed; but she fast outdistanced him.

I sat with my hands on my knees. I raised them, flexed the fingers, placed them back. A fly landed, on the rim of the jug of milk; and I knew I wasn't going to be able to move.

I was still sitting when they came back. For a time, I couldn't raise my eyes above their knees. Finally I made myself look up.

She was shaking, from reaction; her hair across her eyes, a bright bruise on her cheek. Dearbhla supported her, one hand below her elbow; and I never want to be looked at like that again. 'Thank you, Mr Cunningham,' she said. 'Thank you for being so concerned . . .' The other turned her away then. 'Come inside,' she said. 'You must rest, until the doctor is here.'

I stayed where I was. A few minutes, or an hour, later, the harpsichord began to play. The Goldbergs. By then I understood a little better. He never wasted time; so two experiments had been running concurrently. We were the other, the white rats in his maze; his next book would be a treatise on psychology. It would cost him a little paper and ink; it had cost me Sarah.

I walked through. His reflection glowed beneath him, on the parquet floor. I stood awhile and listened, but he didn't turn. 'You bastard, Colin', I said finally. 'You prime bloody bastard.' He did pause at that, hunched his shoulders a little. Then came the little rustlings of the stops; and he began, gently, the tinkling Variation Three. I walked out to the car and drove away; to London, and winters and summers, and a room with nothing in it. A room that would have nothing in it ever again.

And now I suppose I'm going to disappoint you. Within a few months, UK Synthetics merged with the Vogler Corporation of the USA, then with Vancuyck-Coevorden of Amsterdam. And so the mighty InterNatMech was born. Ten years, and the first Synths began to strut; but the answer I needed so badly, that Sarah needed, was never made. Was she a Synthetic, come years before her time; or just some stray Goddess of the courts? Either way, her time of glory was brief; because Dearbhla Cagnac was never heard of again. Though that was hardly my concern. I vacuumed my carpet, and laundered my sheets, and tried to think of nothing, nothing at all.

It was about a year later that I was roused, early one morning, by a hammering at the door. 'Mr Cunningham . . . Mr Cunningham . . . Important visitor to see you!' The voice, the little rising squeak at the end of each phrase, was unmistakable; it was Victoria, the West Indian lass who lived two doors along. I slung a dressing gown on, and opened up.

I was still hazy with sleep; it took a moment for realization to dawn. Finally I said, 'Hello, Sarah,' and she said, 'Can I come in?'

She was pale, her eyes dark-shadowed. She said, 'I've got some bad news for you,' and I nodded. I said, 'It's your mother, isn't it,' and she sat down on the edge of the bed. 'Yes,' she said. 'It was very quick.' She took a handkerchief out, sat staring at it.

I hesitated, looking at my hands. Finally I reached to touch her shoulder. She stiffened; then she flung herself into my arms.

After the storm was over, and she'd washed her face at the handbasin, she said, 'I'm sorry. I swore I wasn't going to do that.'

'It's all right,' I said. 'Come and sit down again. I'll make some tea.'

She touched her nose with the hankie. 'She wasn't a bad woman,' she said. 'She could have . . . got rid of me. After she went away. But she didn't . . .'

'My dear,' I said, 'I never called her bad. I never stopped loving her either.'

'No,' she said, 'I can see that now.' She smiled, wanly, touched her lashes with a finger. God, she was so like her when she did that. 'I was so angry with you,' she said. 'So angry . . .'

'Sarah,' I said, 'she was never really mine. So you weren't either. There was nothing I could do.'

'It's all right,' she said. 'I understand that too. I think I'd have been the same.' She straightened. 'John,' she said, 'you're coming back with me.'

'No,' I said. 'No, Sarah, it wouldn't be right. Not Dorset.'

She swallowed. 'It's a damned great house,' she said. 'I'm not rattling round in it on my own. You don't belong here; and I'm not losing you both.' She stood up. 'I'll come for you tomorrow,' she said. 'Be ready . . .'

I sat on the bed a long time after she'd gone. Then I started to write this down. Because the things inside me had to be given expression; and because the trees across the street were green, greener than they'd been in years. And the last thing I remember is the last thing that she said; standing hand on the doorcatch, with those troubled sea-blue eyes. 'Did it matter?' she said. 'Did it *really* matter?'

It mattered a lot at one time, Sarah. But not any more; not ever any more . . .

THE CHECKOUT

The old lady stood belligerently, glowering round her at the well-stocked shelves of the supermarket. She wore a black and shapeless coat, from beneath the hem of which coyly protruded an inch or two of bright floral apron. An equally shapeless hat of faintly mildewed felt completed her *ensemble*. Her feet, in their black, insecty shoes, were planted a trifle apart; and in one brown, gnarled fist she gripped a heavy stick, which she twitched from time to time with an air of vague menace. ''Arf 'our om bin stood 'ere,' she announced to the air around her, 'and nobody en't bin *neer*. Call this *service?*'

'Oh, Gran,' said Anita, appearing from behind one of the tempting arrays with a well-filled trolley, 'don't be so silly. It's a supermarket, you know that very well. You have to serve yourself.'

The elder Thompson emitted one of her inimitable whoops. Several shoppers faltered, and stared round in alarm. 'Serve *yerself?*' she said incredulously. 'Serve *yerself?* Wot's the world comin' to, I'd like ter know. Very idea, servin' *yerself*. In *my* young days—'

'Well, it was you who wanted to come in,' said Anita, reaching past. Another jar joined the heap in the trolley. Shopping in the biggest supermarket in Kettering had been a mistake in more ways than one; she always had been a sucker for strawberry conserve. 'I told you we'd do better in the village.'

'Well, om a-gettin' *out*,' pronounced the old lady. 'Orl them things there blarin' an' 'ollerin', meks yer '*ead* goo funny.' She glared at the nearest of the wall loudspeakers, from which, interspersed with musak, poured cheerful spiels about the Latest Reduced Lines. 'Ayya got orl them bits?'

Anita pushed her hair back. The day was warm and sticky; and as ever in a town she was feeling niggly and fretful. Her Granny's current mood, culminating in her noisy insistence on finishing the shopping in 'one o' them noo-fangled places', had hardly helped matters. 'I couldn't get any frogs legs,' she said. 'They just don't stock them. Would *escargots* do instead?'

'An' *wot*,' said Granny Thompson fiercely, 'might they be, when they're at 'um?'

'I don't know quite. Snails, I think.'

'Then why dunt they *say* so?' muttered the old lady belligerently. She fumbled in various pockets, failed to locate her glasses and produced instead a much-creased scrap of paper, which she held about a half inch from the end of her nose. 'I esspect we shall atter mek do,' she said. 'No, we kent. *Noot's* eyes, we kent do without them . . .' She peered round as if expecting the absent commodity to materialize before her. 'Dunt tell me they ent got none o' them neither . . .'

'Try the delicatessen counter,' said Anita nastily. Then she gasped. The old lady had set off at remarkable speed for the rear of the premises, where pâtés and gooey cheeses, rollmops and hams and smoked salmon slices displayed themselves in cabinets lit by coldly-glowing fluorescent tubes. Anita pattered after her. 'No, Gran, please! They won't *understand!* It was a *joke* . . . !'

Her Granny waved the list, dancing by this time with temper. 'No *noot's* eyes?' she bellowed. 'No *noot's* eyes? Them there tiger bits I din' 'ardly esspect, not these days. An' snake fillets is 'ard I know, on account o' the winter we 'ad. But call yerselves a *shop*? Everythink, yore supposed t'ev. But you ent wuth comin' to . . .'

'Get the Manager,' said a stout, anxious lady in a bright-checked apron. Anita grabbed her Granny's arm and began to haul her away by main force.

'Dunt you bother,' spluttered Granny Thompson to the small, interested crowd that had begun to gather. ''Cos *I* dunt want ter see 'im. I ent comin' 'ere ner more; an' yer kin tell 'im that from me . . .'

The rest was really all Anita's fault. As a thoroughly modern witch, she always had believed in labour-saving devices. A low-level spell, laid almost one-handed, had rendered the shopping trolley much more manageable. The thing had in fact been driving itself, with only the lightest of touches to steer it round the corners. In her anxiety to reach the checkouts, she clean forgot to degauss the charm; and the trolley, as if scenting victims, accelerated toward an immense, redfaced person in a tent-like floral dress. Anita clapped a hand over her eyes. 'Do like forces *attract*,' she moaned, leafing mentally through her physics, 'or do they *repel* . . .' The matter was rapidly resolved. The clash of metal was followed by a flash of bright blue light; the second trolley shot off in a parabolic fashion, shedding its topload of vegetables as it went. A small man reeled backwards, felled, it seemed, by a cabbage; eggs by the dozen met sticky collective dooms; the immense lady, arms whirling, sat down decisively in the narrow bit by the first of the checkouts, where she instantly became irretrievably wedged. At which point the manager appeared. Anita had never really believed the thing about banana skins; as it turned out though, it was exactly true. He shot past much in the fashion of a water skier, emitting a thin, high wail of despair; and a large stand of Cut Price Lines disintegrated, like metallic hail.

'Oven stuff,' yelled Granny Thompson, struck by a sudden thought. 'That there oven stuff, gel. We need it fer the *catalyst* . . .' She darted aside; then paused, glaring up at the nearest of the offending loudspeakers. Anita whipped her spell-arm down; but for once she was a fraction too late. The assaulted machine whooped to itself, emitted a loud crack and a cone of bright yellow smoke. The effect sped on round the walls of the great shop, unnoticed in the still-growing din; till a stray charge bridged a gap and the burglar alarms set up a merry and gigantic clamour. Instantly, and with appalling speed, the chain reaction spread outside. It had all proved too much for the posse of discouraged dogs who usually sat tied to the rail by the door. Boxers and Alsatians put their heads back and howled; and a Basset Hound broke his lead and bolted. A small car screeched to a halt; behind it, a large green United Counties omnibus did not. The world became a place of crunching metal and rolling, jangling hub caps; and Anita leaned against the wall and covered her eyes once more. Far off, her keen ears had detected a distant *bee-bah, bee-bah* sound. Perhaps it was the police. Or the fire brigade. Or both.

Granny Thompson had finally, after much fruitless fumbling, located her glasses. She perched them askew on the end of her nose and peered at the scene of carnage with every appearance of bewilderment. 'Lor-a-daisy,' she said at length. 'They must 'ave orl gorn orf their 'eads . . .'

'Well,' said Granny Thompson complacently, 'I still dunt see wot it was orl *about*. Allus did think that Ket'rin' was a bit funny. Now I *knows* it . . .'

Anita brushed at her skirt and snorted. 'Well, I think we were lucky not to get arrested.'

'Arrestid?' said the old lady in great surprise. 'Wot *for*? *We* 'adn't done nothink. It were that there manager bloke wot started it, knockin' orl that stuff down uvver. It ent safe I dunt reckon, none on it. *Supermarkits* . . .' She snorted. 'Then that there gel a-sniftin'. Wadn't no call fer that . . .'

'It wasn't us, Gran,' said Anita. 'I've never *seen* anybody so unhappy, her vibes were *awful*. There's something terribly wrong, I'm sure of it . . .'

'Yer kin say that agin,' said the old lady grimly. 'An' I knows wot *with* . . .'

The bus ground to a halt; and Anita manoeuvred the large shopping bag from under the stairs and jumped down gratefully. She set off down the rutted track that led to Foxhanger Copse, towing it behind her. Out of sight of the main road she stopped and took a breath. A quick pass, and the air around the basket became full of little twinkling lights. The thing rose to shoulder height, uncertainly at first; then oriented itself and zoomed off through the trees like a small, somewhat oddly shaped helicopter. She watched it go, then ran to the old lady. 'It's no good, Gran,' she said, 'I shall have to go back.'

'Back *weer*?' said Granny Thompson suspiciously.

Anita tossed her hair. 'To Kettering, of course. Probably this afternoon. I want to find out just what's going on.'

'Ent you ever 'ad enough?' groaned the elder Thompson. 'Orl that squawk an' kerfuffle; you wot *started* it orl, it were. Run y'in next time, put odds on it. An' *I* shent bale yer . . .'

But the accusation, unfair as it was, fell on deaf ears. Anita was wholly preoccupied. Girls with violet eyes and brown hair to their waists shouldn't have to sit at supermarket checkouts. And they certainly shouldn't *weep*. 'She's super,' said Anita breathlessly. 'Sort of mediaeval nearly, I've never seen anybody *like* her. An' working in a place like that . . .' She opened a gate. 'I shall have to borrow Jarmara,' she said. 'Or one of the little ones, the ones that can creep under things. I've got to find out exactly who she *is* . . .'

'Linette Hope,' said Anita, chin in her hands. 'That's lovely too, it really *suits* her. And she lives near Cransley somewhere. Leastways that's the bus she catches an' she only buys a tenpenny. She's supposed to be on some sort of training scheme, she was only supposed to be on checkout a week. But they won't let her off, they say she isn't good enough now. And it's driving her *crazy*, she's really *intelligent*, she's worth so much more than that. The others say she's stuck up an' it serves her right, two of them were talking in the lunchtime. But she's *not*, she's *not*. An' she daren't leave because of getting another job, her father says he wouldn't keep her, he'd put her in the *street*. He sounds absolutely *awful*. An' she can't get a flat or anything because they don't pay her enough. An' the other girls all hate her, they positively *hate* her. Just because she's pretty . . .'

'Wot stuff an' nonsense you do sometimes *tork*,' snapped Granny Thompson irritably. 'Bin' pitchin' yer a fine yarn, she 'as. An' yer've *swallered* it . . .'

'She hasn't,' said Anita, stung to the quick. 'We haven't exchanged a single *word* . . .'

'Well, yer'd better soon start,' snarled the old lady. 'Sooner yer start, sooner yer'll find *out*. Linette this an' Linette that, mornin', noon an' night. Allus were mooney, yer were; if it wadn't this, it were that. An' if it wadn't that, it were *summat else*. An' yer dunt git no better; yer gits *wuss*.' She wagged an ancient and lumpy finger at her granddaughter. 'There's more ter that, my gel, than meets the *eye*. I knows these 'oomans; an' they ain't wuth both'rin' with, none on 'em. Om tole yer times enough; but yer dunt ever *learn* . . .'

'She *isn't* human,' said Anita defensively. 'She's more like one of *us* . . .'

Granny Thompson flung down her crochet work and grabbed for the evening paper. 'While we're *on* the subjick,' she said, 'not as we're ever *orf* it, wot's orl this in the Tellygraph, about 'em 'avin' to 'ave the rat blokes in?'

Anita peered at the headline. PEST CONTROL OFFICERS VISIT LOCAL SUPERMARKET, it said. She swallowed. 'It wasn't anything really,' she said. 'It was just that Jill got spotted. It wasn't her fault,' she went on quickly. 'I know what she's like, but she really was working *hard*. An' there was this great lout of an assistant trying to *hit* her with a piece of *wood*. So Jarmara just *had* to run between his legs, she didn't even *bite* him. Then Lin saw Sugar climbing out of her handbag an' nearly had a fit; an' that scared Jill so she went up the Manager's trouser leg an' . . . I mean, you can't *blame* her,' she finished lamely. '*Can* you . . . ?'

Her Granny moaned. 'Operatin' Familiars without a prior Orthority,' she said. 'Get us both struck orf yer will, then weer shall we be? Yer knows wot they're like, since they 'ad that there *compooter* . . .'

Anita frowned. There was justice in the old lady's complaint, she realized that. These were hard days for a freelance witch; all operations were supposed to be cleared in advance by Central now, and sometimes it took weeks. 'Well,' she said, 'we shall have to do *something*, Gran. They've got this awful down on her, just because she's a girl. That Manager's a beast as well, you should hear the way he sometimes talks to her. If we're caught I shall just have to put it down to Private Research . . .'

Granny Thompson looked up sharply. '*Wot* were that, gel?' she said.

Anita looked puzzled. 'I said I'd have to put it down to Private Research . . .'

'No,' said the old lady testily. 'Afore . . .'

'What? Oh, about Lin. I said they pick on her because she's a girl. There's laws about it now; but they just don't take any notice . . .'

A certain light had come into the old lady's eyes. 'Gel,' she said thoughtfully, 'I dunt reckon as 'ow that's fair . . .'

'Gran,' breathed Anita in disbelief. 'You're a Womens' Libber!'

'I dunt know about that,' said the old lady sharply. 'I dunt 'old wi' them noo-fangled notions, an' well you *knows* it.' She cast around her. 'Git me that jar o' jollop orf the *shefferneer*,' she commanded. 'An' that noo book, that one wot come *Toosdey* . . .'

'But Gran,' said Anita, 'what about the Clearance? You know what you just said . . .'

Granny Thompson gimleted at her. 'If I wants ter do a bit o' Privite Reserch,' she pronounced, 'it ent nobody's affair but *mine*. Om gotta keep me *mind* active, en' I?'

'Gran,' said Anita some time later, 'what are you *doing*?'

Her Granny held a small vessel to the light and stirred vigorously. She took out the teaspoon, shook it; and the bowl drooped in a rubbery sort of way from the stem. ''Ackles a bit,' she muttered. She added three drops of darkish liquid from a vial; the potion gurgled and began to emit puffs of steam and a far from aromatic smell. 'I dunt *'old* wi' folks bein' passed *uvver*,' she went on. 'So we gotta attract some *attention* to 'er, ent we? If more guz through 'er till than anybody else they'll *atter* notice 'er, *wunt* they?'

'I don't know,' said Anita slowly. 'It sounds all right, I suppose it'll work . . .'

''Course it'll work,' said Granny Thompson emphatically. 'Dunt yer trust yer ole Gran ter be right? Not even *yit*?'

'Of course, Gran! But—'

'There ent no but about it,' said the old lady, immersed once more in her book. 'Now let me see . . . Git me them there *hiscargots* out the pantry. I reckon they'll come in 'andy arter orl . . .'

Anita was thoroughly lost. 'But Gran, what *is* it?'

'*Ferry-moans*,' explained the old lady with some pride. 'Jist found out about 'em, they 'ave. Orl them scientist blokes. Jumped-up bits o' kids most on 'em, reckon they knows the lot. But they ent 'ardly started . . .'

The kitchen table was covered with vials and bottles; it seemed the entire stock of the potions cupboard had been called into use at one time or another, Anita had never seen such a complicated spell. Also there had been much chanting and drawing of cabalistic signs; both witches had been kept more than busy. But the brew was finally finished. Granny Thompson held it up. 'Well gel, wot do yer think?'

Anita took the tiny vessel carefully. Mysteriously, the potion seemed to have shrunk during manufacture; her Granny had explained it away airily as 'a controlled *foosion* process.' Now there didn't seem to be more than a thimbleful; but it was very magic. Tiny tides moved in it, little coruscations of light played across its surface. Anita sniffed cautiously. At first there was nothing; just a sweet, powerful scent that reminded her a little of sandalwood. There *was* something else though. She inhaled more deeply; instantly she was falling head over heels through space, accelerating faster and faster to a very strange destination indeed. She rocked; her Granny snatched the little vessel away and by degrees the room stopped spinning round. Anita swallowed, sat up and wiped her face. 'Gran,' she said in a small, admiring voice, 'that's *awful* . . . !'

Linette Hope could never work out afterwards just how she got to be in Deadman's Copse. She didn't even know at first that was its name. She ran out screaming when it all just got too much, and she thought she got on the Cransley bus but obviously she couldn't have because this one brought her in the opposite direction, right up by Wicksteed Park. Then the conductor came and said that was as far as she could go and she hadn't got any more money because she'd left her purse behind; so she just jumped down and ran as fast as she could, not looking back. When she did look round the road was out of sight. Before her a long swell of land was crowned with trees; she walked on into the little wood, not caring. The trees were hung with fresh spring green and birds were singing everywhere, but it made her feel worse than ever.

It had been a bad day right from the start. There had been a row at breakfast, a really awful one, the worst so far; she ran out of the house, walked halfway to Kettering before the bus caught her up. Then Mr Foswick said he couldn't have her at the checkout in jeans, what on earth was she thinking about coming to work like that, so there was another scene. They were lovely jeans too, new and dark blue and flared and bottom-hugging. But she still had to borrow an old frock from another of the girls and it was miles too short and they all started laughing, she nearly walked out there and then. Then the strange girl came in, the one who always seemed to be watching her. She was very pretty, she had brown hair and dark blue eyes and a really super figure, but she stared so hard sometimes it made Lin feel uncomfortable. She was nearly the first customer; and something got spilled all down the side of the checkout, she said it didn't matter but the girl still ran away. She didn't look back but Lin knew she was laughing too. Then the rest all started.

She didn't realize at first, just thought they were busy for a Monday. She kept her head down and worked the till as fast as she could but the noise kept growing till suddenly she looked round. The other checkouts were deserted, the whole line of them; Mrs Creswell and the rest sat glaring and tapping their fingers. Behind her though was this enormous crowd, getting bigger by the minute. They were fighting each other too, all trying to be first; fists and feet were flying, bottles and cans raining down all over. It was like about fifty rugger scrums all going on at once. Others were running in off the street; then Mr Foswick got through somehow with his collar pulled all out and his tie up round one ear and started shouting about it being the Last Straw, and not putting up with any more of it. Then this woman started yelling about who did he think he was trying to take her turn and all the rest started off as well and she quite lost sight of Mr Foswick under the heap of bodies though she could hear him shouting from time to time and making gurgling noises. Mrs Creswell had been rammed into a shopping trolley somehow and couldn't get out, she was making an awful row and kicking about and cannoning off shelves and things. Then the police ran in and they started on them as well and she left the till and everything all unlocked and fled; and now she was here and she could never go back and the world had collapsed into little tiny pieces.

She looked up. She had reached the foot of a great gnarled oak tree crowning a little knoll. It seemed the king of the place almost; but it didn't care about her. Nobody cared about her, not in the whole wide world. She flung itself down by its huge, spreading roots and began to cry. The sobs got louder; and her shoulder was touched. She sat up wildly, glared round ready to bolt; then her face changed. '*You*,' she said bitterly. 'What do you want now? Just leave me alone . . .'

Anita swallowed. 'I'm sorry,' she said. 'I only used a few spots too, I didn't realize. Gran did say it was strong . . .'

Lin jumped to her feet. 'So it *was* you,' she said furiously. 'I knew it all along. An' I suppose you set those rats loose too . . .'

'They're *not* rats! It was only Jill an' Jarmara, they're nothing *like* rats. They're nothing like *anything* really,' said Anita. 'They're my Familiars . . .'

Lin clenched her fists. 'You must be mad,' she said. 'And now you've played this trick I can't go back, not ever. I'm going to drown myself or jump off a building, I haven't decided yet. An' I hope you'll be *satisfied* . . .'

'But we were only trying to help—'

'Is *that* what you call it,' shouted the checkout girl, chest heaving. 'I'm glad you *told* me . . .' She started to run. 'I don't want to *see* you again, not ever. If I do I'll . . . I'll kill you . . .' She vanished among the trees.

There was something decidedly odd about the wood. It had seemed small enough when she entered it, but now it was endless. She walked and walked, for hours it seemed; and rage gave way to tiredness. She finally came to a little stream. The water looked cool and inviting. She drank from it, hoping vaguely it would give her typhoid. A little farther on she reached the edge of the trees at last. Beyond was a broad sunny meadow. A small whitewashed cottage sat peacefully, smoke rising from its chimney. In front of it she saw the brook again, winding between low banks. There were stepping stones, round which the water chuckled pleasantly, and a clump of twisty old willows. By the first of them a pretty, brown-haired girl sat on the grass, her head in her hands. Beside her, anxiously, squatted a sleek Siamese cat. From time to time he put his paw on her knee, peered up to see into her face. Lin approached, soundlessly.

'But Winijou,' the brown-haired girl was saying, 'you just don't *understand*. She's *beautiful*. An' when I saw how sad she was I wanted so much to help. An' . . . now she hates me, she said I got her sacked, an' she'll never speak to me again an' . . . I want to *die* . . .'

It had come to Linette that what she had decided earlier on was true. Nobody *did* care, nobody in the entire world. She had no friends at all now, except one. And Mr Foswick slowly vanishing under a flood of excited ladies really had been very funny. She sat down beside Anita. 'It's all right,' she said. 'I'm not mad at you any more. Whatever it was you did, I know you were trying to help . . .' She felt in the pockets of the borrowed dress, and found a tissue. 'For heaven's sake,' she said, 'this isn't doing anybody any good. Just *blow* . . .'

'She's super, Gran,' said Anita enthusiastically. 'I've never met anybody *like* her. She's so clever, she knows about absolutely everything. She was going to University, she was going to do History, only her father said they couldn't afford it, she'd got to earn her keep. That's what's so *awful*. But she still knows about . . . oh, Kings an' that, the Crusades, *everything*, she's lent me some super books. Did you know you can tell how old a hedge is by the trees that grow in it? It's *fascinating* . . .'

You can tell how old a hedge is by asking the creatures who live there, or divining the nobbly roots of the hawthorn itself; but Anita, it seemed, had conveniently forgotten. She prattled on. 'They've taken her back as well, she was really scared they wouldn't. But the Manager said he didn't suppose it *was* her fault, not really, she was just scared running off like that. She says he isn't really too bad at all, not when you get to know him. She says—'

'Gorn *back*?' said Granny Thompson incredulously. 'Arter wot 'e *said* to 'er an' orl?'

Anita frowned. 'Yes,' she said. 'But you see she reckons—'

'Well, *I* wouldn't,' said the old lady roundly. 'Nor wouldn't nobody with ounce o' self-*rispect*. That there lot orl *chelpin'* at 'er; an' them there things blarin' an' 'ollerin' orl hours, wouldn't stick it five minutes I wouldn't. Ner more would you . . .'

Anita nodded. 'It *is* sort of odd,' she admitted. 'There's masses of other jobs, I looked in the paper, she could do so much better. And she wouldn't have any trouble. I mean, she's . . . well, it would be easy. But when I said about it; Gran, she seemed positively *scared*. An' then she got mad again . . .'

Granny Thompson sighed. 'Om *tole* yer til om sick of 'earin' it,' she said. ''*Oomans* en't wuth a *candle*. There's summat a-gooin' on, my gel, wot you dunt know about. Smart though yer thinks yerself . . .'

Anita bit her lip. 'You're right, Gran,' she said worriedly. 'I know there is, I can feel it. But she won't tell me. Just sort of sheers off . . .'

The old lady sniffed. 'There's *one* way ter find out,' she said. 'If yer *wants* to bad enough . . .'

'I can't *spell* her,' said Anita indignantly. 'An' I promised no more magic . . .'

'I ent suggestin' it,' said the old lady with some asperity. 'Orl om a-sayin', my gel, is that *four* legs is sometimes 'andier than *two* . . .'

'I don't know,' said Anita doubtfully. 'I'm a bit out of practice, I haven't done *that* for years . . .'

'Time yer got yer 'and back in then,' snapped the old lady. 'Or dunt yer reckon yer kin *manige*? Need a bit of *'elp* then, will yer?'

'No thank you, Gran,' said Anita frostily. 'That won't be necessary . . .'

The windows of the supermarket glowed cheerfully in the dusk. It was their late night, they wouldn't close till eight; but the large chestnut-brown cat who sat opposite in the doorway of the fishmongers seemed content to wait. It was a handsome animal, long-haired and with a spotless white bib, of which it seemed inordinately proud. Leastways it glanced down at it from time to time in a pleased-looking sort of way and even essayed the odd desultory lick, as if to ensure that its fur remained immaculately arranged. The street was busy; but for the most part it ignored the passers-by. Once, when a pretty girl stooped cooing, it did condescend to wave its tail and '*prip*' obligingly; but its eyes soon returned to the bright-lit frontage of the shop. Indeed, Lin sat at the end checkout as busy as ever, lifting items from the endless stream of baskets and trolleys, dropping them onto the little conveyor belt, clicking away at the shiny grey till. The cat yawned, and settled down to wait.

At eight the last shoppers were ushered out and a lad came along shooting the bolts on all the big glass doors. The cat became instantly alert. It trotted to the pavement edge, glanced left and right and streaked across the road like a brown shadow. Beside the supermarket ran what the locals would have called a jitty, a narrow alley leading to the car park at the back. The cat paused by the staff door, staring round. A wall, with an outhouse beyond, offered a vantage point. A quick spring, a scraping of claws; and the animal resumed its vigil.

This time it wasn't for long. The door opened and two girls came out together. One was very pretty, with dark hair that hung nearly to her waist. The other, the blonde, must be Josie; Lin had said a couple of times she was the only nice one there. They turned right, toward the Market Place. The cat followed, keeping its distance discreetly; but neither of the girls looked back.

At first it seemed they were heading for the buses; but opposite the Market Place a small, rather depressed-looking pub proclaimed itself the Green Dragon. They glanced up at the sign and seemed to consider; then they vanished inside.

Cats do not frown; but they can certainly look puzzled. Their follower cast about uncertainly for a time; then it sprang to the nearest of the pub's lit windows. It crouched on the sill and peered. Inside, men were playing darts, talking animatedly in a haze of smoke. It jumped down, scurried along the pavement. The second window, muslin-curtained, gave onto a little snug. The girls sat at a corner table, glasses of fruit juice in front of them. Josie was talking animatedly; but Lin just looked dejected. She shook her head, and the other girl began again. The cat craned its neck; but the traffic noise from the road, and the chatter of the other customers, masked the voices.

It also masked the approach of a small, seedy-looking man in overcoat, muffler and battered cap. Nor did he at first observe the animal on the sill. Then his eyes, which were small, rheumy and set rather close together, lit up at the prospect of sport. 'Whurrup' he intoned to the rangy dog that skirmished at his heels; and the lurcher, thus encouraged, flung itself forward with a heart-stopping roar.

Few animals, however, adept, can run up plain brick walls. But cats *in extremis* are capable of remarkable feats. The intended victim gained the top of a little dormer window, from which it spat and lashed its tail, glaring at the hunters as they ambled away. In time its nerves stopped jangling. At least it was safe enough here; and it could still see into the street. It blinked a few times, muttered to itself and settled to watch the moon rise over the great spire of the Parish Church.

The clock chimed the hours and quarters; and the 'tail' was dozing pleasantly when voices sounded from below. It came round with a start, effected a hasty and spectacular descent. The girls had parted company already; Josie was striding off toward the bus stops, but Lin was heading back into the town. The distant chimes struck ten as she turned in beside the supermarket. She didn't stop but headed on, toward the car park.

Her follower, by now, was both puzzled and alarmed. A hasty casting round; and it sprang onto the flat roof of the cold store, where fat ventilators emitted muffled roaring and a gale of warm, meat-flavoured air. It ran to the concrete edge, peered down. It saw the door of the place pop open, the square, foreshortened figure of a man emerge. Keys jangled; and a shadow detached itself from blackness, ran to him. 'Oh, James,' it said, 'It's been so *long* . . .' The silhouettes blended; a sound like a little gasp, and Lin spoke again. 'Please,' she said. 'Oh, please, let's get in the van.'

The cat stayed frozen where it was, struck dumb, it seemed, with shock. Then its neck, which had extended concertina-fashion, contracted with equal suddenness. It blinked and swallowed, as if unable to believe the evidence of its senses. It jumped down, padded forward stiff-legged toward the rusty van parked by the supermarket wall. Scrapings sounded from inside, a muffled bump. The springs creaked faintly; then Lin's voice came once more. 'At last,' she whispered. 'Oh, at *last* . . .'

The miles are nothing to a fleeing cat. London Road, the Park, passed like things in a dream; Kettering was lost over the horizon before it paused. It pounced then, in a wild red rage, on a fieldmouse that in another life had been its friend. It ate it, snarling, all but paws and tail. Later, it was very sick indeed.

Once, when Linette talked, the old fields of Northamptonshire had come alive. She knew everything about the Middle Ages; sowing grain and building churches, Dancing Manias and the Black Death, the Plague Stones where they threw the coins in vinegar. But that was over now, over for good. 'It *isn't* what you're doing,' shouted Anita. 'It's *not*, it's *not*. It's the sordidness. Doing it in a grotty old *van!*'

Lin faced her, truculent and tearstained. 'Things *are* sordid,' she shouted back. 'Everything's sordid, sordid and hateful. Life's sordid, haven't you found that out yet? Don't you know anything at all?'

'But he's *years* older than you! Years and *years! That's* why your father gets mad! I suppose that's why you didn't go to College!'

'Yes,' screamed Linette. 'Because he had me when I was *fifteen* and he's been having me ever since and I don't *care!* And it's nothing to do with you and I hate you, I always did, I shall never speak to you again. You're just like all the rest. You think you're something special, but you're *just like all the rest . . .*'

'But I'm *not*, Gran,' said Anita desperately. 'She said the most awful things, that I was . . . jealous, an' selfish, an' I only ever thought about myself, never her . . . An' it isn't *true . . .*'

Granny Thompson sighed, and laid her crochet work down. 'Gel,' she said to the air, 'the times om *warned* yer. But it ent fer them, it ent ever bin fer them. It's fer *you . . .*'

Silence. The old lady cocked her head. 'Anita?' she said. 'Gel?'

The air of the sitting room swirled, almost made a shape. There was a sob. 'I *loved* her,' said Anita. 'She was my *sister . . .*'

'An' then yer found it wadn't like that at *orl*,' said the old woman gently. 'An' yer didn't want no *sharin'*. Gel, I *knows* yer, yer done it orl afore. Gel, that's 'oomans for yer. Choppin' an' changin' they are, orl on 'em, kent sit still a *minit*. 'Ere terday an' gorn termorrer. Though I esspect yer kent 'ardly blame 'em fer that . . .'

In the corner of the little room, a vase of new green beech leaves trembled violently. 'You're right of course,' said Anita sorrowfully. 'I know that really, deep down. I've been a beast . . .' The twigs shook again; and suddenly there was power. Granny's hair crackled; a small, slumbering Familiar woke and fled squawking. 'Satan spare us,' groaned the old lady. 'Weer's the gel orf to *now . . .*'

Anita's voice shrilled, distant in her mind. 'I'm going to

see her, Gran,' she said. 'I've got to put it right. This very minute . . .'

Linette sat up in bed with the covers pulled to her chin. Her eyes were large and her face was still a little pale. 'Well at least,' she said, 'I know you're . . . not an ordinary person now. But what on earth's *wrong*? It must be the middle of the night . . .'

'It is,' said Anita shortly. She scotched on the bed. 'Look, Lin, I've been absolutely rotten to you. Skulking about like that an' following you, an' then the things I said . . .' She swallowed. 'It was all true,' she said. 'What you told me. Every word. Will you . . . forgive me? Please? I really want to help . . .'

The other girl set her lips. 'You *can't* help,' she said. 'Nobody can. There's nothing to be done at all . . .'

'But there is, I'm sure there is. There must be something. But I have to know . . . all about it first. Lin, won't you *trust* me?'

Linette shot an alarmed glance at the door. 'I *can't*, we shall wake my Dad up. He's ever such a light sleeper . . .'

Anita grinned. 'Not tonight he isn't,' she said. 'Lin, *tell me* . . .'

Lin gulped in turn. Then it all came out with a rush. How you see somebody in the street and it doesn't matter at all at first except you can't quite get them out of your mind. And then you meet and talk and after that you just can't keep away, it's like a magnet pulling. And you try to stop it but you can't, it grows and grows and there's nothing you can do; and everybody tells you, your parents tell you and all your friends, and you're throwing your life away but it doesn't matter any more, nothing matters except that you're with the person and when you're not you're aching right inside, all day and all night too. Till you get an awful job, an awful terrible job, and knowing they're close sometimes helps a bit even if you can't see them. And you nearly come to hate them too but by then it's just too late, it's like a sort of drug, you've got to have them all the time, be with them. 'Like on the films,' said Lin with bitterness. 'It happens on all the films, it's supposed to be nice then. Well, it happens sometimes in real life too. Just sometimes. Only then I suppose it's more a sort of disease . . .'

'Don't say that,' said Anita, appalled. 'Don't ever say a thing like that again . . . Lin, why can't you just go off? You know, do a bunk?'

'Where to?' asked Linette, starting to cry a little. 'We haven't got any money, either of us. We couldn't go abroad; so wherever we went *she'd* find us. James' wife. He married her in London, when he was living there; and he didn't want her then, he told me so. She got him with an awful beastly trick, kept telling him she was pregnant. Now she wears *curling papers*. And she's been foul to him, she found out all about us early on, somebody saw us in a pub one night, you know what Kettering's like. And he doesn't like the supermarket either, he only stays there 'cos of us. He's an under-manager you see, there aren't all that many jobs. He had his own firm once, he was working with his Dad, only they went bankrupt, that's why he came down here, he said if you can't break it up you've got to join it . . .' She smiled, wanly. 'Amazing,' she said, 'the works of a modern supermarket. I think they call them Human Interest Stories . . .'

Anita frowned. 'There's only just one thing,' she said. 'I'm sure of *you*, I've never really had any doubt. But are you sure of him? I mean, it would be terrible. If . . .' She let her voice tail away.

Lin looked serene. 'I could *show* you,' she said, 'only it's getting late . . .'

'As a matter of fact, it isn't,' said Anita airily. 'I stopped Time for you, that's why your Dad can't hear us . . .' And so the board came up, the floorboard under which Linette had stored her treasures, the silver dog-brooch that showed he was a faithful Knight and the *triskele* that hadn't brought much luck and all the rest, the silly things that matter most of all, the skipping rope made from Real Jute and the blue clockwork penguin who could swim in a bowl of water and the furry toys she couldn't have on the dresser, and the vibrator he had given her for when it got really bad, which Anita dropped when its purpose was explained as if it had suddenly got hot. But Lin just laughed. 'It's the eighties now,' she said, 'you have to learn to live with things like that. They'll blow us all up soon; then we won't have to worry about anything, will we?' She opened a little album. 'Look,' she said, 'that's me at the seaside. We actually went away for a whole weekend once; I said I was staying with a friend from school, and James was on a Course. And that's us playing tennis, and that's us on the Links. . . .'

Anita frowned at a colour Polaroid. 'Lin,' she said, 'what's this?'

Linette peered. 'Oh, that was a party we went to years ago. Everybody was in fancy dress.'

'So *that's* James,' said Anita. She was excited now. 'He's got a super face . . .' He had too; not handsome but sort of *broad*, with long-tailed greeny eyes. 'It *suits* him,' she said, hardly believing. 'It's just right, he's a Mediaeval man . . .' A huge idea had dawned. 'Linette,' she said, 'I *can* send you away. Both of you. Somewhere nobody would ever find you again . . .'

'But there *isn't* anywhere. I *told* you . . .'

'There *is*,' said Anita, breathing quickly. 'There *is*. And it isn't very far away at all . . .'

Lin looked uncertain. 'Would I be able to . . . see you?'

Anita set her mouth. 'No. But that doesn't matter. You'll *always* be my sister, nothing can change that now . . .'

Linette put her face in her hands. 'I wish I could split myself in two. So one of me could stay . . . Anita, you're the b-best friend I ever had . . .'

'Nonsense,' said Anita briskly. Then it got to her as well and she took Linette in her arms. 'You'll have to be ready,' she said. 'James too. I want you to come to a party. A *fancy-dress party* . . .'

Linette jumped back. 'I couldn't, I just couldn't. I'd s-spoil it for everybody else . . .'

'You *wouldn't*,' said Anita fiercely. 'Lin, it's the only *way* . . .'

'The Great Charm,' whispered Anita. 'Please Gran, just this once. You and Aggie could do it, I *know* you could . . .'

The old lady looked uncertain. 'Well, I dunno, gel,' she said. 'Kent do *that* without a Clearance, that's fer sure. An' they wunt *give* it.' 'Elpin' 'oomans, wotever next . . .'

'But Gran, don't you see? We'd be helping them to *sin*. Damning their immortal souls, an' all that rot. They couldn't *refuse* . . .'

Her Granny looked up sharply. 'Gel,' she said, 'I never *thort* on it like that. I reckon it'd work . . .'

★

Party invitations are always exciting to get. But when they're brought by a seal-point Siamese with a collar of tinkling bells, they're things of wonder. Lin gripped James' hand the tighter, feeling her own heart thud. Winijou was still ahead of them somewhere, he'd met them at the road. Only now he seemed to have vanished. She ducked under low branches. Despite the times she'd been, she was still not sure of Foxhanger after dark. It was all right though, because there was another cat. Large and stertorous this time; and though the moonlight made it hard to tell, it seemed a very odd colour indeed. It arched its back and spat; but it too waved them on. And there was light at last, two twinkling spots of fire. Gateposts had been set up in front of the cottage; on top of each sat a portly little dragon, who sparked up if he thought you needed it. James drew back; but Linette laughed, feeling excitement go to her head like wine. 'It's all *right*,' she said. 'Oh, do come on . . .'

She'd given her dress an awful lot of thought. Great ladies wore veils and hennins in those days, and girdles at their hips and lovely gowns; but she was no great lady, she was a checkout girl. So she'd come barefoot, in russet. There were flowers in her hair though; and James looked good as well in his jerkin and leggings and funny nightcap hat.

Anita met them at the door. She never had been able to pass up a chance, the things she'd done with ermine were beyond belief. Lin swallowed, and dropped low. *'Mi levdi'* she whispered, right in her part already; but Anita pulled her up, laughing. 'Come *on*,' she said. 'Everybody's here, I want you to meet them *all* . . .'

Surely, thought Lin, she must be dreaming already; because the cottage wasn't a cottage any more, not once you got inside. An ox was roasting in the Great Hall, the spit turned by some highly improbable Things; and candles, hundreds of them, were making a mist of light and musicians were playing high up on a gallery, strange instruments that wailed and bonked above the roar of talk. 'These are my friends the Carpenters,' shouted Anita. 'This is Charles and this is Sir John, he's really very famous. John, that tabard's *great*, it's really *you* . . . An' these are my cousins from Northampton, an' this is Mr MacGregor, he's a really super vet, an' this is Ella Mae, she's flown from

America specially. I mean Long Strand, where all the Indians are . . . An' this is Mr Strong, he's come all the way from Dorset . . .' And on and on; Lin had lost track before she was halfway through.

'Gran said to say hello,' yelled Anita, even louder than before. 'Only she can't come for a mo', she's busy with the spell . . .' And certainly from a side room were coming rumblings and concussions, interspersed with irate shouts. 'Aggie, kent you even *count*? . . . Well yer'll *atter*, I kent find me *glasses* . . .'

There were goblets of wine, great tankards of mead and beer. Lin's head was spinning before they danced *La Volta*. Then the figures swirled into fresh and stately patterns; because Time was getting older all the while, and it was a *pavane*. 'For a dead princess,' gulped Anita, the wine making her light-headed. Her hand touched Lin's, the last time ever; and suddenly there was nothing. Just the two of them, and a funny sort of mist.

Lin dropped to her knees. She said, 'Where's *James* . . .' and Anita laughed. 'It's all right,' she said. 'He's here . . .'

Lin stared round her, at the silence. 'What's happened?' she asked dazedly. 'Where's the *spell*?'

Anita laughed again. She said, 'You're right *inside* it,' but the other shook her head. 'It was just a party,' she said. 'It was lovely; but they always end the same.'

'Not this one,' said Anita. Her eyes were glowing strangely. 'Come outside . . .'

They followed her, stood staring. The woods looked different somehow, in the early light. The bushes were coppiced, as they used to be; great mounds of leaves made homes for creeping things. And it was quiet, so quiet; not a sound, in the whole breathing world.

Lin's voice was very small. 'Anita . . . where are we?'

Anita smiled. 'Near home,' she said, and pointed. 'There's a big hill over there. One day they'll build a town on it called Kettering. It'll have supermarkets. All sorts of funny things . . .'

It was a tiny whisper. '*When* are we then?'

Anita swallowed. 'They'll fight Agincourt tomorrow,' she said. She turned to James. 'You'll be one of the Gentlemen Abed. But I don't suppose you'll mind that at all, will you? I wouldn't . . .'

She pushed her hair back. 'You don't *have* to go,' she said.

'You're still being *shown* . . .' She hesitated. 'It wasn't . . . all maypoles an' dancing, you know. People . . . didn't live that very long . . .'

She'd already seen the look in his eye though. He rubbed his face, and spoke for the first time that whole night. 'But how we'll live, girl,' he said huskily. 'How we'll *live* . . .'

Anita touched the great quiver of arrows on his shoulder. 'You're not James any more then,' she said to him. 'You're Jack the Fletcher, an' this is your lawful Wife. Her name is Linet . . .' She couldn't stand any more then, so she ran away. Because that's how it has to be when you really have a friend. You love them as hard as you can; and then you let them go.

When she looked back they were already running down the slope. Linet turned once, she thought she saw her wave; then the morning mist had swallowed them both.

'Checked out,' whispered Anita. She sat a long time with her head down; but when she straightened up her face was calm. The cottage was making itself again behind her, like a pale blue picture of a house; and Kettering forming, far off on its hill.

THE COMFORT STATION

She came over the skyline cautiously, ducking among the low gorse clumps that dotted the hillside. Between the spiny bushes with their bright haze of flowers were outcrops of rock, orange-patched with lichen. She dropped prone by the tallest of them, wriggled forward to lie staring down, her chin on her wrist.

Below her, some fifty metres away, ran a narrow metalled road. By it the first of the stones stood like sentinels in a bleached sea of grass. The lines stretched into distance, ragged and broken. Beyond, the plain ran to a blue horizon. Closer at hand a coppice thrust out an arm toward the road. Where road and trees met stood a foursquare little building of fawn-coloured brick. Beside it was a metalled parking area, empty of cars.

The girl ran her tongue across her lips and studied the building. It was flat roofed; it possessed two little skylights, and round the walls were narrow windows of muffled glass. Two doors, both open, faced the road. Beside each, fixed to the wall, was a square white plaque. Each had a black doll-symbol on it; a man, and a woman. A breeze stirred the branches of the trees. Nothing else moved, and the afternoon was silent.

She wiped her forehead with her arm. She stared behind her, then back down. Her eyes were large and wide-set, of a colour between green and brown. Her face was broad across cheekbones and jaw, her skin tanned to a clear light olive. Her hair was dark. A strand blew across her mouth and she put it back without removing her gaze.

She waited some time by the rocks. Finally she rose. She stared behind her once more and started down the hillside, hobbling painfully. She wore a faded khaki shirt and light belted slacks, grass-stained about the knees. The shirt was marked with sweat, between the shoulder blades and under the arms. A canteen bumped at her hip; on her back, held by a broad sling, was an automatic rifle.

At the road she paused again, staring right and left before

limping across. She flattened herself against the wall of the little building. She took the gun from her shoulder, eased through the nearer of the doors. Inside she straightened slowly, staring once more; at the line of cubicles with their blue-painted woodwork, the spotless sinks, the towel unit showing a loop of crisp white linen. The brick walls were painted a cool grey; and at the rear of the place was another door, also blue. She edged forward, touched the catch. It opened. Beyond was a narrow room, likewise unoccupied. She saw a tall cupboard, a rack of slatted pine shelving. The uppermost shelf held spare rolls of towel; everywhere else, on the floor, piled on the shelving, were cans of beans and spaghetti, corned beef and stewed steak. She opened the cupboard. It was full as well. She said, 'Jesus Christ.'

Outside again, the sun struck hot. She leaned on the wall for a moment, holding one foot away from the ground; then she repeated the exploration. The men's side was empty too, smelling of disinfectant. The little windows were propped open on stout brass stays; the urinal gleamed whitely, the copper pipes above it polished to a salmon pink. About the place was the hiss and tinkle of water.

At the back an identical door led to a second storeroom. There were more shelves, also piled with provisions; a chair and folding table, saucepans, a twin ring camping stove, a sink. The window was open; she craned, saw the nearest of the trees. Beyond them the stones shimmered in sunlight.

In one corner of the little room was a camp bed heaped with blankets. She laid the gun down and sat on the edge of the bed, gripping her ankle. She swung her legs up, lay back and closed her eyes. It was her intention to doze, rest a few minutes before moving on; but a deeper sleep claimed her.

Her waking was instantaneous. She jerked erect, scooping up the gun in the same movement, sat glaring at the man who stood in front of her.

He was short, and balding. He wore an old check shirt, the sleeves rolled to the elbows, and a pair of baggy corduroys. On his feet were boots with brightly polished toecaps. His fringe of hair was browny-grey; and he wore hornrimmed spectacles through which he blinked, eyes sidling away and back. One hand was still on the catch of the door; in his other he held a bulging carrier bag.

She lowered the gun, slowly. She said, 'You must be the Attendant.'

He didn't answer; and after a while she said, 'What's in the bag?'

He shuffled forward a little, back hunched. He gripped the bag, protectively; and she repeated the question. He started at that, eyes flickering. He dropped the thing on the table, with a quick little movement. Some of its contents spilled; and she laughed. 'Mushrooms,' she said. 'I expect the woods are full of them.'

She swung her legs from the bed. 'You gave me a scare,' she said. 'What's your name?'

No answer. She stared, curiously. She said, 'You can talk, can't you? Do you understand what I'm saying?'

He opened his mouth, as if to answer, but no sound came out. A tic developed in his cheek; and she shrugged. 'Forget it,' she said. 'It doesn't matter. Have you got any cigarettes? Cigarillos?'

He stood puzzling, as if coming to a momentous decision; then he shuffled across the room, still with his eyes on the bunk. He took down a carton, opened it and laid a pack of cigarettes on the end of the bed. She grabbed for it, disbelieving; and he jumped back.

'It's all right,' she said. 'I shan't eat you.' She opened the pack, hands shaking a little. She produced a lighter, flicked it. She inhaled, and blew smoke gratefully. She said, 'Thanks . . .'

She laid the pack down. 'Did you see anybody in the woods? Any soldiers?'

He shook his head, frowning. She watched him for a moment with her brilliant eyes. 'I'm Anna,' she said. 'Not that it matters.' She paused. 'There were twelve of us,' she said. 'They jumped us, early on. At first light. I got away with a twisted ankle. The rest . . .' She stared, at nothing. 'You're sure there wasn't anybody?'

He still stood, it seemed undecided; and she lay back on the bed. She said, 'God, I could use a drink.'

He didn't react immediately; just glanced under his brows, at her, at his hands, at the mushrooms scattered on the table.

Finally he turned to the sink. He filled a kettle, set it on the little stove. He produced a box of matches and lit the gas, placing the spent match carefully in a round tin lid. She said, 'This is crazy.' She pushed her hair back. 'You lost your electricity,' she said. 'But you've still got water. That I can understand. There's nobody else to use it.'

When the kettle boiled he took down a teapot. He warmed it, spooned in tea and stirred. He produced two bright, thick beakers, filled them and placed one on the table with a bag of sugar. Then he stepped back.

'Okay,' she said. 'It's all right.' She got up, limped to the table, took the beaker and returned to the bed. 'I expect you're wondering about me,' she said. 'I'm the last thing you expected to see. Well, I'm wondering about you too. You been here all the time?'

No answer.

'Do you *know* what happened?' she said. 'To the town? Or did you just think it was some sort of fancy firework show?'

Nothing.

She nodded. 'You knew,' she said. 'That's why you stocked up. Where'd you get it? Village near here, is there? With a shop?' She looked round her. 'Must've taken you a month,' she said. 'Hauling it all back. You've been real busy, haven't you? Why'd you do it? To stop yourself thinking? Or wasn't that ever a problem?'

She drank the tea, slowly, and set the mug down. She said, 'That was good.' She glanced at him. 'Have you got a bowl? I want a bowl of cold water.'

When he did decide to move, it was always suddenly. Like a bird. Or a lizard. He scrabbled in the locker beneath the sink, straightened up with a yellow plastic bowl. He filled it and turned to her, looking troubled.

'Over here,' she said. 'Put it on the floor.'

He did as he was told, and scuttled away again.

'You're not a deaf mute,' she said thoughtfully. 'You're just scared. What of? I'm not going to hurt you.' She bent to unlace her boot. She pulled her sock off, wincing, inspected her ankle. It was puffy and inflamed. She rolled her trouser leg to the calf, lowered her foot carefully into the water and began to bathe it. 'I planned on moving out by nightfall,' she said. 'But I'm not going to get much farther on this. So it looks as if you're stuck with a non-paying guest.'

The other glanced at her shyly, and back to the table. Then it seemed he once more reached a decision. He took down a saucepan and began peeling the mushrooms, carefully, inspecting each one before dropping it in. 'That's fine,' she said. 'You just carry on with the housework. Don't mind me.'

She lit another cigarette. She said curiously. '*Did* you get out? When it started? Or was this your job all along?'

The other set the pan on the gas ring and turned the flame low. He added oil from a plastic bottle, and a plopping and crackling began inside.

'All along,' said the girl. 'That's my bet anyway. And you just stayed put. You reckoned it was the safest place. You fetched the stove, and the food, and the bed. So you could sit it out. It was easy, there was nobody left to stop you. Or maybe you didn't reckon anything. You just couldn't think what else to do.'

The other unzipped a tin, added its contents to the pan. The sizzling redoubled; and the girl put her head on one side. 'You been a Shithouse Dan all your life?' she said. 'Or did you come down in the world?' She showed her teeth. 'Maybe it was what you wanted,' she said. 'A nice little number. Your own boss, and nothing to think about. And what the hell's wrong with that?' She looked thoughtful. 'I wonder how you got the job,' she said. 'Somebody knew somebody? Or was there an advertisement? Who'd you have to write to? The Council? Or the Museum?' She shook her head. 'It's things like that I always want to know. The little things. You can't ever know enough. Not if you live a million years.' She stubbed the cigarette. 'Sounds crazy, doesn't it?' she said. 'Living a million years. But you know what Alex used to say? There's nothing to it. A million people do it, every twelve months.' She moved her foot, carefully, and winced again. 'They killed him this morning,' she said. 'Got him through the legs. They didn't waste any more bullets though. And it wasn't quick either.' She swallowed. 'I had to watch,' she said. 'I was up among the rocks. I couldn't get away because of my ankle.'

The Attendant set out two plates, and turned off the gas. The girl watched him, broodingly. 'All for you,' she said. 'Do you know that? That's why he died. That's why they all died. So we could give back what they took from you. Only we were wasting our time. We can't give back what you've never had.' She smiled lopsidedly. 'It doesn't make any difference to you,' she said. 'You've always been here, haven't you? Like the stones. You always will be. You're *Homo sapiens*. With your head in a bog and a flute stuck up your arse.'

The other turned to her, blinking.

'All right,' she said. 'Okay. So you're doing your best. With what the good Lord gave you.'

He filled a plate and held it out to her. She stared at it. 'Funny,' she said. 'Thinking about eating.' She looked up. 'I think I was in love with Alex,' she said. 'But you can never really be sure, can you? The more you think about it, the less you can tell. We used to screw a lot. But that doesn't prove anything. Now I'm eating again.' She toyed with the food. Finally she pushed the plate away. 'They cut him,' she said. 'Where it hurts. And staked him out. I hadn't got the gun. Not then. Afterwards I thought I was going to have to finish it off. But there wasn't any need.'

The sun levelled, pouring light through the westward-facing window. The Attendant stared at it, and at her. Then he produced a shiny bunch of keys. He shuffled out and she heard the windows being shut, the doors locked. When he came back she laughed. 'You're still keeping time,' she said unbelievingly. 'Toilets open eight a.m. to sunset. You know something? You're through your skull.'

She looked thoughtful. 'No,' she said, 'let's work it out.' She stared at him. 'You were always slow, weren't you?' she said. 'I can see you at school. Sitting in the corner hoping nobody would notice. All hunched up with your glasses. You didn't look any different. Even then.' She paused. 'What were your folks like?' she said. 'What did your father do?'

No answer.

'He didn't earn much,' she said. 'Or they'd have made something of you. Maybe he worked for the Council. Is that how you got the job? Somebody was sorry for him? He must have been disappointed . . .'

She looked round her. 'This place hasn't been up all that long,' she said. 'What did you do before? In a factory, pulling handles? Or maybe you weren't even smart enough for that. Maybe you swept the floor. And made the tea. You'd do that well. But you wouldn't get any thanks. They used to get on to you, didn't they? Yell at you. Because you were thick. They were still sending you for lefthanded screwdrivers when you were forty. They'd think that was funny. And your mother kept house and tried to make the money go round. Did you have any brothers and sisters?'

The other moistened his lips and shook his head fractionally.

She shrugged. 'Well,' she said, 'it wouldn't have made any difference. Your life's the only one nobody could write. Because nothing happened. You never had a girlfriend, did you?'

He winced, and turned away.

She laughed. 'No,' she said, 'you wouldn't have got to first base there. You're one of evolution's dead ends. Well, I'll let you into a secret. It's your nails. They've always been black, haven't they? And we don't like black nails. We think about the foreplay.' She leaned back. 'Nobody ever told you that, did they?' she said. 'And it's a bit late now. But they say it's never too late to learn.'

She lit a cigarette. 'What did your mother say, when you got the job? Or maybe she was dead by then. Had enough. Maybe they'd palmed you off onto an aunt.'

The other frowned. His lips moved, forming a word.

'Auntie,' she said. 'We're making progress. You were living with an auntie. You didn't like that either, did you? But you'd found a way out by then. You'd got this job. It was all you ever wanted. You could open the doors and shut them and polish the pipes and scrub the floors and it was yours. All yours. You were grateful, weren't you? Really grateful. That's why you're keeping it up together. In case they ever come back. They won't; but you're not to know that.' She shook her head. 'Maybe you'd got the bed here before the bombs,' she said. 'They were just a relief, weren't they? They meant you didn't have to go back any more. Get underfoot. Or maybe you just liked the stones. Is that it? Do you like the stones?'

His eyes flickered toward her and away.

'No,' she said. 'They don't mean anything to you. Why should they? They don't mean anything to anybody. It was this. The quiet, and being on your own. You'd given up worldly things. They got too much for you.' She laughed again. 'You know what? You're a hermit. Or a Saint. Did you ever think of that?' She shook her head. 'I can see the attraction,' she said. 'The shadows moving round, and the clouds. And the cistern flushing, filling itself back up. It wouldn't do for me though. I haven't got that sort of patience.'

She stubbed the cigarette. 'You'd got it made,' she said. 'Then I turned up. Threw it all out of gear. You don't know what to do about me, do you? You don't have any idea.'

She fell silent, in the growing dusk. The other looked toward her, and away. He picked at his nails, self-consciously; then frowned, fell to scratching at a food stain on his shirt. Finally she moved. She put her sock on, carefully, laced the boot. A shelf beside her held a stack of blankets; she took them down, inspected them and rolled them into a bundle. She said, 'I'm going to get some sleep. But not here. This isn't your lucky night.' She held her hand out. She said, 'Give me the keys. To the other side.'

He drew back.

'Yes,' she said. 'That gets to you, doesn't it? Like asking for your glasses. They're all you've got, you're no good without them. But I still want them.' She snapped her fingers. '*Keys* . . .'

He jumped. Then he put his hand into his pocket. He took out the bunch of keys, divided it clumsily. He pushed the smaller set toward her and drew back again.

'Thanks,' she said. She stared down at him a moment longer, the gun on her shoulder. Then she turned away.

He waited, huddled in the chair. He heard the outer door of the place open and close; and a footstep, distant and light. Like water. He moved then, quickly; ran to the party wall and crouched by it, head bent as if listening. But there were no further sounds.

When it was almost full dark he took the candle from one of the shelves and lit it. He found a square of cardboard, pushed it into the aperture of the single window. He lifted the bunk blankets then, and pulled out a scrapbook. It was dogeared and much thumbed. He crouched with the candle, and began to turn the pages.

He woke at first light. He walked through the Station and unlocked the outer door. Mist was lying waist-high, across the road and between the stones. He stared at them awhile, then turned and plodded in the opposite direction.

Deep in the wood he paused. There was a scuffling, at the foot of a gnarled, spreading tree. He stooped. The wire had taken the rabbit by the back legs. One of them was all but severed; round the wound the fur was dark and clotted. He found a stone, smashed the creature's skull with it. Then he took a penknife from his pocket. He paunched and skinned the animal, haggled its head off. He wrapped the meat in a square of sacking and stood up.

The rest of the snares were empty. He retraced his steps. By the time he reached the edge of the wood the sun was breaking through. The mist layers shone golden though the Station was still in shadow. The girl was coming out of the door. She had the gun on her shoulder and was carrying her shirt in her hand. Below her neck her body was much paler. Nearly white.

On the fringes of the wood the bracken fronds grew graceful and tall, nearly as high as his head. He ducked back, into the concealing green. She stared, it seemed straight at him; but she didn't enter the trees. Instead she moved away along the edge of the copse. He followed, at a distance.

On the far side of the tongue of trees was a little hollow, bright now with sunlight. Beside it another of the outcrops of rock. She spread the shirt out on it, and other things. She sat down beside the rock, her back to him and her arms round her knees. She didn't move again.

It was midday when she returned. She had put the shirt back on. The stew was simmering on the little gas ring. She sniffed appreciatively. She said, 'Something smells good.'

The meal was ready by the evening. She ate, it seemed with more appetite. When she had finished she lit a cigarette. She said, 'I was thinking. About what I said. It was nearly the same for me. I was a teacher when it all started. I didn't know what I wanted either.' She blew smoke. 'Aren't you going to tell me about yourself?'

He shook his head. He had never found much use for words. They betrayed him constantly, stumbling and slithering, out of his control; now, there was no help in them. He risked a glance at her. Her hair looked different somehow. Shinier. She flicked it back. She said, 'I saw you in the wood this morning. Did you see me?'

He turned away. He felt his face burning, and his ears. He collected the dishes and began to wash them. She laughed. 'You'll have to get used to it,' she said. 'Happiness is a clean pair of knickers.'

He bit his lip, and nearly dropped a plate.

She stuck her foot out. 'My ankle's much better today,' she said. 'Look, it's not half as swollen.'

He darted a glance, still fumbling with the cloth.

She stood up. 'I'm going to walk,' she said. 'Just as far as the stones. Do you want to come?'

He shook his head, confused; and she shrugged. She said, 'I just don't think you want me around.'

He watched her surreptitiously, from the window. She had the gun on her shoulder again. She never went anywhere without it. She crossed the grass to the first of the stones. She put her hand out curiously, touched the lichened surface. Then she squatted down, sat staring fixedly towards the south.

There were long cloud streaks on the horizon. The sun dropped behind them and darkness came quickly. He stared till he could no longer see her. Then he turned away. He put the square of cardboard over the window and lit the candle. He stood a further time undecided. He took the keys from his pocket, frowned at them, put them back again. Finally he went to the bunk. He glanced round him; then took the scrapbook out, settled with it on his lap.

She came back so quietly he didn't hear her. Not till the door opened. By then it was too late. His hands darted, left and right; he lost the precious second it would have taken to hide the book again.

She said curiously, 'What was that? What did you put under the bed?'

He made a noise.

She held her hand out. 'Come on,' she said. 'It can't be all that terrible. Let's see how you really spend your time.'

She walked forward, reached to the blankets. He scrabbled; and his hand brushed her forearm. He jerked it back instantly, as if he had received an electric shock.

She stared at him. She said, 'What a funny little man you are.' She lifted the blankets, unopposed, withdrew the book. She opened it. For a moment she looked baffled. Then she began to laugh. 'Southsea, 1979,' she said. 'Couldn't you find anything better than that? And look at this one. Come to sunny Eastbourne . . .'

She flicked through the pages. The bikini girls smiled back at her, from brochure covers, fading, ill-gummed newsprint. She shook her head. 'At least they're all brunettes,' she said. 'Shows some taste I suppose . . .' She put the thing down. 'Well,' she said, 'so much for Saintliness. What was the matter? Daren't you buy Playboy?'

He stared at the floor, trembling.

'Just a minute,' she said. She picked the book up again, sat at the table. She leafed through it more slowly. 'There's something about them,' she said. 'It's more than just the hair. They're all a type, aren't they? You collected them for years . . .' She narrowed her eyes. 'What were you doing?' she said. 'Trying to remember? Was there somebody, once? Somebody you knew? Who was she?'

No answer. She hardly expected one.

'No,' she said. 'Nobody you knew . . .' She put her head on one side. 'Someone you saw,' she said. 'Maybe only once. Where was she? In a car? On the beach?'

Nothing.

'Where was it?' she said. 'Was it Southsea? Is that why you kept the brochure?'

The Attendant began to exhibit signs of distress.

'Southsea,' said the girl. 'How old were you? Twelve? Thirteen? Were you there with your parents? Perhaps it was the daughter at the digs.' She started to laugh again. 'I can see it all,' she said. 'You poor little bastard. Pulling your winkle, trying not to get it on the sheets. Nothing you could do, was there? It's things like that that start Revolutions. And it stayed in your head too, didn't it? All those years, buzzing around.' She stared at him. 'What did you do instead? To get your mind off it? Collect seashells? Watch the ships?' She closed the book, sat a moment thinking. 'Look,' she said finally, 'won't you tell me? Get rid of it? You've never had anybody else who'd listen. But I will.' She paused. 'You could get it off your back,' she said. 'It's been there long enough. You really could be a Saint then.'

A silence, that lengthened. Then she sighed. 'I don't expect you can,' she said. 'Not after all this time. It's part of you, isn't it? Like an animal. Always running round the same little track.' She stood up and shouldered the gun. 'I only came back because I'd run out of cigarettes,' she said. 'Can I have some?' The other didn't look at her; and she walked to the shelf, took a packet from the carton. She stared at him once more, and went out. The door closed behind her, silently.

She found him next morning squatting among the stones. He tensed when he saw her, and for a moment it looked as if he was going to bolt.

She said, 'Hello.' She squatted down beside him. 'I looked all over for you,' she said. 'I thought you'd done a bunk.' She pulled a stem of grass, and leaned back. 'I had a funny dream,' she said. 'About the stones. I came out and the road had vanished. And the woods. Nothing there at all. Just the stones; and sort of rolling clouds. We were marooned. Crazy, wasn't it?' She grinned. 'Heloise and Abelard,' she said. 'Modern style.'

He sat frowning, head turned away, picking at the grass beside him with little nibbling movements of his fingers.

She sucked the straw, thoughtfully. 'Look,' she said finally, 'I'm sorry about last night. It's not your fault. You can't help being a victim of Advertising. And I'm sorry I laughed. It wasn't at you though. I don't suppose you'll understand it, but I was laughing at God.'

He made no response; and she tried again. 'Look,' she said, 'I know it isn't easy for you. I'm her again, aren't I? All the faces come together. After the first few years. But I'm not her really. I'm just somebody passing through.' She wriggled her foot. 'I shall be moving out tomorrow,' she said. 'I wanted to leave you with something better than that rotten little book.' She sighed.

'You must have had your chances,' she said. 'Everybody has their chances. Why didn't you take them? We're all alike really. If you turn us bottoms up.'

The wind rose, moving the grass with its bobbing yellow heads.

'It's not easy for us either,' she said. 'I know you don't believe that. But it's true.'

The silence extended; till, suddenly it seemed, she became aware of the oppression of the megaliths. Their weight, the massiveness where they leaned and crouched in the grass. She said, 'Perhaps you were right all along.' She sat up, arms round her knees. 'Look at the stones,' she said. 'Look at that one there, it's as big as a house. And the one next to it. The pillar. Have you noticed they're all in pairs? The pillar, and the big flat diamond?' She shook her head. 'You couldn't get away, could you?' she said. 'Nobody gets away. Even here. There's only one Secret. In all the world. The stones know it. And so do you.'

In the afternoon he wandered, deep into the wood. He didn't want to be near the Station. Neither could he go away. He felt tethered, like a dog. Dusk was falling when he returned, the mist already starting to make its shapes among the trees. The Station was empty, and his room. He stood on the carpark undecided; hesitant, rubbing his head, blinking, taking little short steps forward and back. Finally he scratched at the storeroom door. It was a little noise. Ashamed, like a mouse.

She opened it. He waited, hanging his head. She said, 'You got your courage up. I wondered if you might. It isn't any use though.'

He raised his eyes, then flicked them aside. Her shirt was unfastened, right down to her waist.

'It's all right,' she said. 'I don't mind you looking. It's all you can do, you poor little sod.'

He twisted his hands together.

'Look,' she said, 'I'd like to take it away from you. For good. But I can't. Don't you see that?'

His face twitched. He didn't look up.

She shook her head. 'You don't believe me, do you?' she said. 'Then I'll show you.' She moved forward. She took his hand, guided it under her shirt, made the fingers knead and press. 'You've never done that before, have you?' she said. 'Just dreamed about it. But you're doing it now. Is it nice?'

He snatched his arm back, suddenly. He stood gripping his wrist, staring at his fingers.

'I told you,' she said gently. 'You're a bookworm. It could never be any good. It would never have been any good with *her*. Do you understand now?'

His voice, when he finally used it, was thick and creaking. Like the earth. He said, 'Goodbye.'

She leaned toward him. He felt her lips brush his forehead. 'Don't look for me in the morning,' she said, 'I shall be a long way off.' She touched his hands. 'Goodnight,' she said. 'Happy dreams.'

She closed the door and leaned against it. She rubbed her face, squeezed the bridge of her nose. She rolled the blankets for a pillow and lay on her back, staring up at the ceiling.

Her own sleep was disturbed. She turned and threshed, woke to hear an owl call above the woods. Finally she dozed. When she opened her eyes again the little window was already showing blue-grey light.

She got up and buttoned her shirt. She walked through to the Station, used one of the cubicles. She washed her hands, ran her fingers through her hair. She filled the canteen and slung the automatic onto her shoulder. She stepped outside yawning, walked round the front of the building. She paused, staring across to the stones; and a foot scraped behind her.

She said, 'You're up early.' Then her eyes dilated. She flung herself to one side, clawing at the gun.

The noise of the shots startled birds up from the wood, rushed out huge across the stones. Concrete chips flew, the fawn brick was pitted. She yelled; and galvanic reaction carried her through the doorway. Silence returned.

The man lowered his gun. He was tall and broadshouldered, with a dark blond stubble of beard. He wore the remnants of a khaki uniform; on his head, set aslant, was a battered forage cap. He glanced behind him, gestured and edged forward.

She was sitting against the first of the cubicles, her shoulders pressed to the blue-painted wood. Her hands were to her stomach. She had dropped the gun; it lay six feet from her, in the middle of the floor. She saw the soldier dimly, bulky as a bear. Behind him hovered the Attendant. She rolled her head at that. She whispered, 'No. You couldn't . . .'

She tried to move; but her legs, it seemed, would no longer obey her. At the third attempt she rolled over. She began to work her way across the floor, hotching on her elbows. Behind her she left a lengthening dark puddle. The soldier waited till her fingers touched the butt of the automatic; then he shot her unhurriedly through the heart. He walked forward, scooped the gun up by its strap and slung it on his shoulder. He turned away then, without a word.

It was an hour before the Attendant returned. He edged round the door and stood a long time watching, his hands behind him against the wall. He crept to her, finally. He rolled her over, tried to lift. But she was heavier than she looked; and her head would loll, her eyes stare so. Finally he fetched a scarf, with which he blindfolded her. He set her upright, puffing, began to drag her toward the door. Her heels extended the puddle, waveringly; outside, the marks lost themselves on the asphalt. He looked round him, blinking in the sunlight; then began to move again, jerkily, across the carpark to the fringes of the wood. Where the bracken spread its bright green fronds, closing him from view.

The shadows were lengthening before he reappeared. He seemed dazed; and his walk was unsteady, so that as he reached the doorway of the Station he put out a hand to steady himself against the jamb. He walked to the first of the basins, began to wash his arms. Then it seemed he became aware of the state of his clothes. He whimpered, and ran into his room. He reappeared wearing a fresh shirt and trousers. He crossed to a locker, blue-painted like the rest, took out a bucket and mop. He worked methodically, swabbing the edges of the great pool, changing the water often. He finished finally, emptied the bucket into the channel; and the urinal flushed, with a steady hissing. The last of the stain swirled away; and the cistern began to refill.

He put the cleaning things back into the cupboard. He walked round, locked both outer doors. He pushed the square of cardboard over the window, and lit the candle. Crockery lay in the sink; he washed it, setting the cup and plate she had used carefully to one side. He whimpered again, formally; then he curled up in the corner with his book.

THE CASTLE ON THE HOOP

I've been with Fitzsimmons for years; most of my life in fact. I remember it as a pretty run-of-the-mill Midlands ad agency; but then, Northerton is a pretty run-of-the-mill sort of town. We had a studio manager of sorts, a girl to do the pasteups, the odd Improver, an old biddy to keep the guard books; and that was all the troops we needed. Any decent jobs that came in, we usually farmed the artwork. All that changed though the day we hooked a million pound account.

How we did it would make a story on its own; but I haven't got room to set it down here. Suffice to say that it was a pretty hectic time. Toby Warrilow, with whom I suppose I've had a love-hate relationship for years, set about servicing it; the MD's ulcers developed ulcers, even I got a little ragged at the edges. And I've been in the game for—well, longer than I care to set down here. Things sorted themselves out finally though; the account was running smoothly, or as smoothly as these things ever run, and Toby proposed a trip to Town. He had some artwork to drop off, and a couple of quick calls to make; after which, as he said, the day would be our own. Which sounded very much all right to me.

The authorities, in their wisdom, had started yet another campaign against the twentieth century; life for the motorist, as we rapidly found, had become very much a case of staggering from one dog pound to the next Dallas clamp. We gave up finally and dumped the car, tubed down east to the Tower. We debated whether we'd have time to wander round the new ship museum at St Katharine's Dock, decided we hadn't and headed up toward Billingsgate instead. Toby, who has some odd tastes for an account exec., had conceived a desire to see the old Roman bridge abutment before the final concrete was poured. As it turned out, the dig was closed to the public that day. Well screened off too, with high wooden shutters; no way to catch as much as a glimpse. He muttered a bit, but there was nothing for it; the morning was wasting, and I for one was starting to feel decidedly peckish. We walked up to Southwark Bridge, leaned on the parapet for a moment to enjoy the cool breeze from the river. Then Toby set out purposefully again. 'You wouldn't think, would you,' he said, nodding at the concrete jungle ahead, 'that there was an old boozer buried among that lot?' I shook my head, and smiled a bit. I'd known the Angel on Bankside about twenty years longer than I'd known him; after all I was born in the Smoke, earning my living there for years. But there are times when Toby chooses to overlook little things like that. After all, he's nothing if not a showman.

All the same, I was appalled by what was happening; the desolation, the mile on mile of building sites, the new impersonal cliffs of office blocks rising sheer from the water. Not even a towpath, for the common folk, if they still exist, to recreate themselves. So much for inner city planning. I said something of the sort to Toby and he nodded, looking for him uncommonly grim. 'Yes,' he said, and inclined his head again. 'You know what was there of course, once on a time?'

'Yes,' I said. 'The stews.'

I went a bit quiet myself. Somehow it was all in the name. From time immemorial, Southwark was the city's red light district. I'd even heard it claimed there were already speakeasies there when the Romans first came thumping up from the coast. The Crusaders of course reintroduced the heretical idea of occasionally washing the skin; the bagnios were first established in Southwark too, and the old trade received a facelift. Right through the middle ages king after king tried to root out the offence, taxing the licensees out of existence, scattering the Ladies of the Town with swingeing statutes; but they always crept back. Now they were gone for good; their final shroud was of concrete too.

We pushed on, past the sad little memorial that's all that's left to mark the site of the once-mighty Globe. The Angel when we finally reached it was much as I remembered it; the old iron lantern, the funny little half-round doors on the corner, still painted a festive black. Inside of course it's much changed; a complex stack of little bars and snugs, touristy even to the names they sport; Boswell, Johnson, the incredible Mrs Thrale. There's no juke boxes though, leastways none I've ever heard, and no Musak. If you never saw a worse conversion job, you wouldn't come to much harm.

Toby ordered a snack lunch, rather grandly, and a couple of pints. We were served by a lively little lass with a broad Geordie accent and the slimmest waist I've seen in years. It was quiet there for a weekday; we talked for a while about things in general, how the new development had affected trade and all the rest. Then she flitted off on some errand of her own, and I smiled. 'Nice kid,' I said.

Toby nodded, sipping at his beer. 'Yes,' he said. 'But she's not a Londoner.'

I frowned. I would have thought that at least was patently obvious. There used to be such a thing, certainly, as a London barmaid; but they're getting to be a rare breed now. Usually, almost anywhere in Town, you're assailed by the dulcet tones of Australia or South Africa. I said as much, and Toby shrugged. 'I knew one once,' he said. 'Use to work here, as a matter of fact. A year or two ago.'

I glanced across at him. He'd been in a funny mood all morning; nothing you could put your finger on, but definitely not his normal ebullient self. 'Maybe she's still here,' I said. 'You could always ask the landlord.'

He nodded. 'She probably is,' he said. 'But the landlord wouldn't know.'

Obviously there was more to come. It was equally clear it wasn't the time for asking. He'd tell me in his own way, or not at all. I ordered some more ale, and we spent a pleasant half hour chatting about Newcastle; the things they'd done to the town, how they'd ripped the middle out to build the rapid transit system that's come to be known locally as the Clockwork Orange. Toby recovered after a time; patted his hair, dropped his voice a notch or so and even conned us a couple of shorts at five past three. Which proved, if nothing else, that the old alchemy did occasionally still work.

We left a few minutes later, walked under the grim old rail arch at the top of Clink Street and down to the Cathedral. The day had grown sultry, the great nave was pleasantly cool by contrast. We spent half an hour there, but Toby was still restless.

We moved on again, wandered down to the Belfast. There he finally plumped down on a seat, and lit a cigarette. We sat and stared at the old ship's high, curiously battered-looking sides, the lines of tourists shuffling up the long gangways from the shore. Finally I said, 'I'm sorry you didn't meet your friend.'

He stared at me. He said, 'What do you mean?'

'The lassie you were talking about. The barmaid.'

He blew a little cloud of smoke. He said, 'You're rather jumping to conclusions, aren't you?'

I hesitated. Usually it's a safe subject for legpulling; after all he's always been one of the world's champion chatters-up. This time though something in his manner warned me I was on delicate ground. 'Sorry,' I said. 'I didn't speak.'

He was quiet again, staring across the river at the line of new, bland frontages. Finally I said, 'What was she like?'

He considered. 'She was tall,' he said. 'Tall for a Londoner, anyway.'

'Well,' I said, 'are you going to tell me about it, or not?'

He shrugged. 'You wouldn't believe a ghost story. Not coming from me.'

'Is it a ghost story?'

He said, 'Judge for yourself . . .'

Those were his great times of course; he's always been a superb exec., and with a million backing him he couldn't go wrong. The night he spent ten K on a dinner party for six, and explained the bill in terms of Kimmeridge Bay lobsters, was probably the high point of his life. Though that time I really did think Clarkey, our MD, was going to join the great Agency in the sky. It paid off of course, eventually; but it was a dodgy deal, even by Toby's standards. It necessitated his continuous presence in Town for three or four months; when he finally condescended to grace Fitzsimmons again he looked as if he'd aged so many years. I'd put it down to the stint of financial juggling; now it seemed it hadn't been his sole preoccupation.

He'd more or less taken up residence in the Tower Hotel, the vast new ziggurat they've piled up on the once-blameless spit of land between Tower Bridge and the old docks. I looked across at it as he was talking, and smiled. I've never set foot in it, but

apparently it's a pretty fair place. 'Better in than out,' he said at
the time; he's always described the outside, libellously, as being
like a kingsize stack of stale Mars bars.

Most evenings, when the latest junketings were over, he'd
walk to clear his head, try and settle his thoughts; up past the
Monument, along to Blackfriars, over the river sometimes into
Southwark. He soon discovered the George; he still sometimes
waxes lyrical about the remnant of galleried yard, the spiced
sausages you could buy there. Then somebody told him about
the Angel; so the next chance he got he bent his steps in that
direction. Nor was he disappointed. There was warmth in the
old place still; a welcome, and good company.

I glanced across to him. 'Was that so important?'

He nodded. Took out another cigarette, sat studying it
absently. 'I was lonely,' he said.

I was faintly taken aback. I'd never associated that sort of
feeling with Toby; Toby the dandy, Toby the man about town.
Which means I still don't think about my fellow creatures half as
much as I should, because it was obvious once he'd spelled it
out. He'd set up the deal to end all deals; his job was on the line,
he knew that well enough. There was more to it than that
though. In the old days, I once worked half a year on a painting.
It was going to be my *magnum opus*; for a time I thought the
Academy was only a step away. Then I looked at it one night
and knew I'd failed. Well, selling was his art form.

He stirred. Lit the cigarette after all. 'It wasn't always there of
course,' he said. 'The Angel. There was an old, old building
once. The Castle on the Hoop. Reckoned that was a sort of
drainage ditch, ran round it like a moat.' He shook his head. '*Ye
Castell on ye Hoope*,' he said. 'What a name for a boozer. Or
whatever it was.'

I nodded, drily. 'Yes,' I said. 'Or whatever it was.' I considered. London is built on layers; dig down and you'll find
them all. Even the stripe of bright red ash that was all that was
left when Boudicca's mob had finished with it. Despite the
battering it's taken from the Luftwaffe and the Developers
though, Southwark is still one of the places where the sense of
oldness comes through strongest. I could almost see them, in my
mind; the line of leaning, shabby inns, the Bull, the Elephant,

the Cardinal's Hat and all the rest, stretching clear to the bridge. Staring up to Westminster, where for generations they picked up their scurrilous trade. Between them the alleys, no more than shoulder width, that ran down into that secret world of pimps, footpads and worse. Behind loomed even older ghosts; the high wall, queer round half-roof of the Globe, flags fluttering on high days and holidays; beyond again the bearpit, chief competitor for old Will's trade. The roars, the bloodlust, echoed over rooftops, mixed with the whine of dive bombers, the rat-tat-tat of guns.

I came round with a start. The sounds came from the Belfast; an audio-visual demo for the hordes of eager children.

'Then they built the Angel,' said Toby thoughtfully. 'The year Bach turned his toes up, that was. Old Thrale was still banging away round the back, trying to bankrupt Colonel Sam. Quite a time, that must have been.'

'You know a lot about it,' I said. 'Did she tell you?'

He frowned. 'In a way,' he said. 'In a way.'

It was a cheerless night, the first time he crossed to the pub. A steady drizzle falling, thin drifts of mist haloing the streetlamps, the lights along the river. He must have felt oddly out of place; the original City gent complete with brolly, tap-tapping his way above the half-seen water. But fires were burning in the great hearths, the many lamps gleamed soft and golden. He admired the big model of the Globe, stared in awe at the vast derelict armchairs scattered about, that have been there ever since I can remember. Then he turned. She was waiting patiently, arms folded; he thought, instantly, how her hair and skin were golden as the lamplight. She wore a soft, casually-buttoned shirt, a long, suedey skirt; and I've no doubt his hand went to his own hair, patted the little quiff he's always been so proud of, his voice dropped that critical notch when he ordered his beer. His boardroom manner, he calls it; though 'bedroom' has always seemed more appropriate to me. He's not a tall man, probably there's some who wouldn't call him handsome; but he has good eyes, big and long-lashed, and he's always known how to use them. She didn't seem impressed though. She fetched a glass quietly, filled it; took his money, gave him his change and resumed her pose, staring beyond him to the windows. The river, and the night.

I grinned. 'So you didn't score for once,' I said.

For a moment an odd look went across his face. There was pain in it, and something like bewilderment. But he merely shook his head. 'No,' he said. 'I didn't score.'

Something still seemed to be eluding me; some fact that, once known, would allow others to click into place. After all, he'd so far said very little. Long shadows seemed to stretch, certainly, from the simple image of the girl, the quiet bar; but they were formless as the rest. 'What was she really like?' I said. 'Can you describe her?'

He hesitated. 'It's difficult,' he said. 'There was a quality. She was . . . broad-hipped. Well put together, good shoulders. She could have been an athlete. A horsewoman.'

'And was she?'

He smiled, briefly. 'Chance would have been a fine thing. Not too many hacking stables, in Bermondsey.'

I considered. I thought I'd grasped, dimly, what he was trying to say. There's a type of girl, not too commonly seen, who doesn't need to speak to make her presence felt. She isn't often beautiful, sometimes she's not even pretty; but when she walks into a room, heads turn. There's a word for it now; vibes. Not the most elegant of syllables, but I suppose they had to invent it sooner or later. She's a woman, certainly. She's also an Immortal.

'What?' said Toby sharply. 'What was that?'

'Sorry,' I said. 'Just a thought.' I hadn't realized for a moment I'd spoken out loud.

He looked thoughtful. 'Funny,' he said. 'It's pretty good really. Sort of sums it up . . .' If there was a thought to finish, he didn't oblige.

It was odd how her image stayed with him; on the long trudge back to the hotel, through the day that followed. And the day after that. Then it was the weekend. He left his problems to simmer, drove back up to Northerton. It was ten days, maybe longer, before he saw her again.

His first impression of her had been of hardness; something in the set of jaw and cheekbones, the clipped, sharp accent when she troubled to speak. That was only to be expected though, from a London lass. In a funny way, they're always in control. If they go out without a coat, it never dares to rain. His second meeting changed the image though. Her eyes were wide and shadowed; they were also haunted.

'Haunted?' he said. 'What by?'

He didn't answer at once; just sat and pursed his lips. 'I never found out,' he said. 'Not properly.' He flicked the cigarette butt away. 'She wore her hair up, in a chignon,' he said. 'She knew it suited her. There were always little wisps escaping though. As if she'd done it in a hurry.' He narrowed his eyes. 'Wore sandals a lot too. But then, you need something easy on the feet. Doing a job like that.'

The second time she talked more. Asked if he was staying up in Town, and where he hailed from. He was faintly surprised. He didn't notice the sandals, till she came round to clear the empties from the tables. After that, they intrigued him. They whispered softly, on the old boards. So many feet, before hers. That was the night he found out about the Castle.

'From her?' I said, but he shook his head. 'I'd picked a couple of books up,' he said. 'It was all new to me. Expected it though, somehow.'

'Toby,' I said, 'you're not making too much sense.'

'No,' he said, 'I know.' He fell quiet again; we both sat and watched the great grey ship in front of us. Something like a bosun's pipe wailed from her; she was welcoming another party of visitors. 'Did she know about Bankside?' I said. 'All the little tarts?'

He shrugged. 'Depends what you mean by knowing,' he said. 'One way, no. She wasn't much for book-learning. Another way, yes. She understood the lot.' He clenched his fists, banged them suddenly on his knees; an odd little gesture, coming from him. 'They wore aprons,' he said. 'And funny striped skirts. A uniform, by Act of Parliament. By fourteen, they were through. Out in the gutter, walking like geriatrics. Faces a hundred years old.'

I didn't know quite how to answer. I'd never heard him speak with such concentrated bitterness before; it was as if the old times were still happening, right before his eyes. But that's the thing about London history of course; it skulks up when you're least expecting it, with a mallet in its hand. I suppose what I did finally come out with was a bit lame. 'Well at least,' I said, 'some things have changed for the better.'

'Maybe,' he said broodingly. 'Maybe not.'

Somehow, I had to make a link. 'Did she feel herself drawn there?' I said slowly. 'Was there a sort of empathy, is that what you're saying?'

Again he didn't answer directly. 'I read a book once,' he said. 'Years back, when I was still a kid. There was this idea about ghosts. About things getting themselves recorded, sort of soaking into the woodwork. I think it's worse than that. I think it comes up out of the ground.' He half-turned, looked back the way we had come. 'I wonder if a yard of concrete will be enough?' he said. 'If that'll seal it off?'

He walked on when he left, along what used to be Bankside. One of the old flights of river steps still remained; the rotten balks of timber leaned drunkenly, out across the water. Farther on was the last of the alleys that had led into that fearsome maze of hovels. It ran down now between two empty, ramshackle houses. They'd slung a door across, to seal it; in Northerton, he'd have taken it for a garden gate. He walked off finally, away from the starting lines of window-sockets. That night he couldn't get warm, in his neatly-coverleted bed, in his centrally-heated room.

The work he'd visited on himself came hard. The girl's face floated persistently before his eyes; the other images that troubled him were more vague. In the afternoon he read, and drank a little whiskey. The last of the stews came down, turned into the warehouses of nineteenth century commerce; but he remained unsatisfied. In the evening he crossed the river, turned down once more toward the Angel. It was the first of many pilgrimages.

That night the old inn was busier. She couldn't have talked much, even had she wished. He sensed in any case the old reserve was back. There was something else too, that he hadn't seen before. A paleness, almost a tension. She picked the glasses up, as she'd picked them up before; brushed past him, sandals lisping. He thought it was maybe her wrong time of the month. The thought surprised him; he wasn't a man to concern himself with things like that. He wondered just how far she'd wound herself into his awareness. And why.

'Why?' I said, and stopped. I'd caught myself on the edge of some flip remark; this wasn't the time for it. I think I had an image of her too, by then; built up in pointillist touches, but an image nonetheless. 'Go on,' I said.

'Go on,' said Toby vaguely. 'Where to?'

'I don't know,' I said. 'It's your story, not mine.'

He wasted an hour of private telephone time. It would be added to a bill that was already far too high; but he needed to hear a Northerton voice. Afterwards he sat and stared at the grey crawl of the Thames. Then he shrugged himself into his coat, picked up his brolly. It seemed a pattern had been set.

A week later she was more herself again. She even divulged the odd few private details; how she had a brother on the boats, the places she'd worked up West, how her mum had started having her on the Southend dipper. He listened and nodded, revolving his own problems. He wanted her out of that place; out of the area, if only for a while. But possibilities were limited. His room, hers? Nothing seemed to suit. He felt disoriented; all his *savoir faire* seemed to have deserted him. And all too soon, the fear was back. Stronger than before.

'What was she afraid of?' I said.

He shrugged. 'The usual stuff. A long black car. A little shiny knife. Sounds a bit Hollywood, doesn't it? When you say it like that.'

I frowned. I'd heard of such things happening up round Soho; not over the river though, surely. Anyway, London's supposed to have been cleaned up. I said bluntly, 'Was she a hooker?'

He shrugged, almost irritably. 'I don't know,' he said. 'Maybe, one time. Maybe she stole from them. Or cheated on her patch. Or maybe she was just trying to get out. They don't forget though. There's always a bill at the end.'

He saw the enemy once. Leastways he took it to be the enemy. Curiously, he couldn't remember afterwards what the man had looked like. He was short, certainly, and powerfully set; he wore a belted, well-cut topcoat and his hair was dark, slicked back. He sat to one side of the bar, toying with a bottle. That one curious fact did stay in Toby's mind. He couldn't remember what the stranger was drinking; but each time he insisted, with an imperious little gesture, that the bottle be passed over for him to serve himself. What he did recall was the blazing white of the girl's face. Once she pressed her hand to the wall, as if to stop herself from falling; once the other touched his tongue to his lips, ran a finger round the bottle mouth with an air of indescribably relish. He tapped the thing then gently on the counter edge, to call for a replacement. At that the others in the bar left silently; Toby was on his own.

What he did next must have been as big a surprise to him as it was to me. He's a connoisseur of punchups; but always on the strict understanding that he's not involved himself. So to walk up to the bar, lean elbows on it and smile down at the other, he must have been in a very strange mood indeed. 'I think,' he said gently, 'that you're rather upsetting the lady. So wouldn't it be better if you left?'

It had been quiet before; but the silence, he said, took on a whole new quality. The fire crackled softly; she turned a stricken face; and the other took his time before looking round. At which point Toby's description faltered again; because although he still maintained he couldn't remember the face itself, he remembered well enough that the smile was returned. It was, he said, the most chilling expression he'd ever seen; because behind it there was genuine amusement. The other picked his hat up, took his time about adjusting it, gave him one more long, quizzical look and left without a word.

'Well,' I said. 'At least you won the round.' But Toby shook his head. 'No,' he said, 'I lost. I'd lost before I started.'

'What did the girl say? Afterwards?'

He smiled. He said, 'Can't you imagine?'

It still didn't seem to be adding up. 'Look,' I said, 'what you're saying is, she'd somehow upset this . . . gang, whatever they were. And they were threatening her. What were they going to do?'

His answer had an almost childlike simplicity. 'They were going to cut her,' he said. 'She didn't want them to.'

The words chilled, momentarily. 'But damn it, man,' I said, 'she could have got out. Anywhere. What was she doing, waiting to be punished?'

He shook his head. 'It isn't as easy as that,' he said. 'I told you, she was a Londoner. I sometimes think there isn't anywhere else. Not for folk like that.'

'I did it,' I said.

'You had a different Path,' he said. 'There's a saying about that somewhere. You can choose to walk in sun or shadow. But it's still the same street.'

I hesitated. Apart from anything else, Toby talking Buddhism was definitely food for thought. 'What did you mean?' I said. 'About losing before you'd started?'

'As she saw it, there wasn't any choice. She said she was a woman, so she was born to suffer. Just like all the rest.'

'When did she tell you that?'

He said, 'A few nights afterwards.'

The deal had been going well. Two days, and he could shake London's dust. It should have eased the tension. Instead, it raised it.

She was resigned now; totally, it seemed. He tried to speak to her once about what had happened; but she merely shrugged. 'It's all right,' she said. 'Don't worry, you done your best.'

It was late; Last Orders gone, Time called through all that stack of bars. She said, 'You'd better come upstairs,' and for a moment he was baffled. He followed her nonetheless, through room after room. He hadn't realized before the sheer size of the place. He said it reminded him of something Mervyn Peake had written. I didn't know till then he'd even read him.

She had a room she sometimes used. If it got too late. Not much of a place; a bed, a wardrobe, a few things scattered about. On the bed was a big Paddington Bear. 'A good one,' Toby said.

She made him coffee, on the little gasring. There was even brandy to follow. She sat and nursed the glass. That was the only time she talked; about the old days, all the folk who'd lived there over the years. That was soon done though. She got up, and kissed him.

It was about the last thing he'd expected. It took me by surprise as well. His amours, after all, have always been strictly private. He's got strong principles about that.

She was warm; also, she was in tears. He pushed her away. He said, 'Nobody can chiv a girl who owns a Paddington.'

I turned and stared at him. At last, I'd understood. I said, 'You poor old so-and-so.'

'Yes,' he said, 'I felt a bit let down myself. She'd slammed the door.'

They threw a party, the day they signed the contract. From all accounts, it was quite an affair. They even hired an Oriental dancer; the TV men dipped pound notes in their champers, tried to stick them on her belly. Toby came away.

He'd been sleeping badly. There was a persistent dream. He wasn't too clear what it consisted of. He said there were voices, a whole lot of voices; they all wanted something from him, but it was something he couldn't give. Because Time had moved on. He was locked in the twentieth century; or so he thought.

He lay on his bed and dozed, but it was no good. The voices were back, more insistent than before; and there was the other thing as well. He couldn't take her to Northerton, not any more. Because she'd go there as a lover. Or a tart. And that, he'd finally realized, wasn't what he wanted. You see although he's been married for years, he's childless. After so long, he was hoist by his own petard. He'd found out what love means; but she hadn't seen it quite the same way.

He got off the bed, and set his tie straight. He took the lift down to the carpark, started up. He wasn't too clear what he was going to do. The thing was over; but he had to see her again.

I said, 'You *drove* back down?' and he said, 'Yes.' It was already twenty after ten; he didn't have time to walk.

I shook my head. It isn't a thing I'd like to try myself, not now they've changed the streets round like they have; and he was probably over the top as well. I said, 'Did you make it?'

The way was blocked, finally, by a pair of artics. He begged and pleaded, got one of them to move. It let the long black car through too. In fact, it passed him.

'*The* long black car?' I said.

He nodded. 'Yes,' he said. 'Just like on the films.'

The rest's even vaguer. He wasn't, anyway, in the most analytical of moods. He saw the pub, the big rail arch; he saw her as well. She was running.

I said, 'They'd come for her?' and he nodded. 'Something had come for her,' he said. He stared, suddenly, at the Belfast. He said, 'Have you ever been round that ship?'

'Once,' I said. 'When she was first moored up. Why?'

He looked miles away. 'There's a chart,' he said. 'Shows the range of her guns. She could lob bricks on Hampstead. Make a nasty mess.'

I was puzzled again. I said, 'Why bring that up?'

He smiled. 'She was here that night as well,' he said. 'She couldn't help. Any more than me.'

One thing, at least, he'd remembered from his schooldays. He knew how to tackle. You go in hard, lock the opponent's knees; that way you stand a good chance of not being kicked in the teeth. He said the guy's skull hit the path with a smack that still gives him a headache if he remembers it; and the car didn't wait for any more. It screeched round in the road, headed back the way it had come. Maybe they thought they'd been staked out.

I said, 'So you got her back?' But he shook his head. 'It was too late,' he said. 'I'd waited just that bit too long.'

The river was high; he'd never heard it make a noise like that. And the night was black as pitch. He turned away from the roaring, still running blind; and finally there was light. He swears it was a cresset; a burning torch, fixed in an iron frame. But that's impossible. It wouldn't have been right, not even for the fourteenth century; it's another touch of pure Hollywood. It let him catch a final glimpse of her though; he thought the skirt she wore had funny stripes across it. But by then he had troubles of his own. The ground underfoot was slimy, he was running ankle-deep in mud. The maze of alleys turned and twisted, no more than shoulder-wide; also it seemed a mob had collected behind him. Maybe he'd alarmed them, by bursting so suddenly into their lives; but the noise they made, the menace, couldn't be mistaken. And they were gaining ground. He glanced behind him, caught the flash of something, he thought it was a weapon; and that was his undoing. There was a flight of steps, worn down and rounded, gleaming with wet; he leaped at them, and caught his foot. The world became a brief affair of whirling dark, then bursts of coloured stars. He remembered, just before he landed, the strange stench of the place; old and sour, sick.

Then there was a burst of even greater sickness; then nothing much at all.

I was quiet for a while. I was wrestling with the notion that somehow or other I'd been had. Toby nodded. 'Yes,' he said. 'I felt the same myself.'

'So what happened next?'

'Very little,' he said. 'When I woke up I was lying in a puddle on a building site. Some guys in bonedomes looking a bit concerned.' He pulled a face. 'I'd ruined a damned good suit.'

'Look,' I said, 'are you trying to tell me . . .' I stopped, and he shrugged. 'I'm not trying to tell you anything,' he said. 'Except what happened.'

I said, 'So where is she now? You must have followed it up.'

He glanced upstream again. 'Maybe back there,' he said. 'I hope the hoods aren't still after her though. She deserves a bit of peace. They all do.'

I've always been stubborn. I don't know whether it's a virtue; but at least it's a fact. I said, 'Are you telling me she really did vanish?'

He nodded. 'Her parents were nice folk,' he said. 'It cut them up a lot.'

I gritted my teeth faintly. 'So what's your answer?'

'I haven't got one,' he said. 'Just one or two ideas.' He considered. 'There was a magician once,' he said. 'Used to make his living bending spoons. Then a lot of kids tried it for kicks. One or two of 'em found they could do it for real.' He paused again. 'If you were scared enough,' he said, 'could you bend Time?' He saw my face change, and forestalled me. 'All right,' he said, 'so she belonged with the other lot. Years back. And they called her. Does that suit any better?'

The sun was lower; and a little breeze had risen. It struck with an odd chill; and suddenly I saw him shiver. I stood up. 'Best get moving,' I said. 'It's still a fair step back.'

As we left the wharf, the playback from Belfast was starting again. Her last show of the day. In a way, I was glad to leave. Somehow, I wouldn't care to be on her after dark. Too many ghosts.

DIVA

*(A small tale meant for whispering aloud, in the accents of
the South West Highlands).*

It was in the summer of nineteen thirty five that the then Lord
of Ardkinross—Willie the Tenth, as he preferred to be known
among his more intimate associates—set about the conversion of
his home into a centre of culture and a theatre for the staging of
operatic performances. At the same time I, Jamie MacLachlan,
was engaged as gardener and general assistant to the Laird; a
position I have held ever since, with the exception of a brief
interruption caused by an Austrian corporal of somewhat dubious
lineage.

His Lordship was spurred on in his endeavours by a vast
contempt he had conceived for a not dissimilar institution in the
south of England, which in his hearing at least it was always best
to leave nameless. The origins of the dispute were never made
wholly clear, although a tale did circulate at the time of a fracas
over whether or not the kilt could be considered proper evening
apparel in Sussex. I incline to the belief that it may have
contained a kernel of truth, as Willie's first decree was that the
kilt and the kilt only would be worn to Ardkinross performances;
a fancy that could not however, be sustained, for lack, I suppose
one might say, of general support.

Though his Lordship's love of the performing arts was perhaps
exceptional his business acumen was not, having been inherited
from a line of worthy forebears. Thus performances at Ardkinross
commenced in the forenoon, what Willie described as 'the meat
o' the day' being occupied with charabanc trips through the
surrounding countryside, which is of course well known for its
wild and rugged beauty. Since the region is equally noted for its
hospitality, audiences could be guaranteed to return in a tolerably
receptive mood; and since the Laird maintained an interest in
each of the establishments at which the visitors had paused, the

project enjoyed considerable commercial success. The fame, not to say notoriety, of the Ardkinross Interval spread far and wide, eclipsing finally that of its despised rival, a visit to which could offer little more than the delights of a picnic supper; a practice His Lordship characteristically condemned as effete.

Willie the Eleventh inherited both his father's business flair and his passion for the arts. Ardkinross was redesigned, the lines of sight improved and an hydraulic stage installed, complete with lifts and other devices for the furtherance of visual effects. It proved itself ideal for performances of such sagas as the Ring, although the night young Hamish MacDougall was given charge of it a new dimension was added to the concept of *Hochdramatische*. The Magic Mountain reared abruptly from the steepness of a gable roof to something approaching the vertical, causing the world-renowned Siegfried to slither incontinently into the orchestra pit. Still, as Willie later observed,the incident at least afforded him the opportunity of proving his professionalism to the hilt; like the trumpeter in the play, he held his note to the end. The ultimate blame could in fact have been laid at His Lordship's door; Hamish had been doubling as coach driver that . day and had partaken, not wisely but far too well, of the facilities provided for the guests. He was assigned to other duties, and clauses written into subsequent contracts governing in some detail the employment of stage machinery during performances. Willie, who has a golden tongue in him when occasion demands, managed to soothe the ruffled feelings of the actor, who had somehow contrived not even to break his neck; and the affair was passed away, though I must confess to a certain lingering doubt as to its accidental nature. Not, you will understand, that anything was said as such; but Hamish did later confide an opinion to me that the piece was 'monstrous overlang.'

In order to finance his increased activities Willie embarked on a campaign to promote world-wide sales of the family whisky; the renowned Glen Ardkinross, hitherto the sole province of connoisseurs. He took himself off to London for the purpose, procuring the services of an establishment specializing in such matters; after much discussion, what I believe is termed a 'pitch' was agreed upon and he returned well satisfied. He remained in that enviable condition, though I will own to certain feelings of misgiving when the first of the advertisements finally appeared. It may perhaps be a slowness of perception, but I have always failed to see the connection between scantily clad young females and the selling of any commodity, least of all malt whisky. The wording equally left much to be desired in terms of taste; at one point it even seemed to hint that the beverage possessed therapeutic properties in certain areas I had hitherto considered, and continue to consider, private. His lordship though was wholly unrepentant. 'Whisht, mon,' said he, clapping me on the back in the way he has, 'It's nobbut a *deveece*. And it's for Ardkinross; all's fair in love, war and opera . . .'

I have not infrequently heard puzzlement expressed at the numbers of the famous who have seen fit to grace our remote corner of the Highlands. The answer is one that lies deep in the soul of any truly great man or woman; they come for the money. And if Willie had been openhanded before, he now became prodigal. The season at Ardkinross eclipsed, I think, all others. Day and night, the glen rang with the sound of voices; the strains of the orchestra floated fulsomely across the lawns; the single road by which the village is approached was crammed with motor cars and charabancs, to the vast and continuing irritation of the local sheep.

Not, you will appreciate, that His Lordship's generosity could be said to be wholly impartial. Local tradesfolk had been heard to describe him as being on the canny side, while with head gardeners and the like he could be positively thrawn. Nor was he drawn overmuch to producers, directors, designers, theatrical agents, stagehands, dressers, prompters, repetiteurs, conductors and musicians in general; in fact he did confide to me once that he feared there might be a danger of his becoming eccentric. His love was reserved for the singers; the basses and baritones, the tenors and countertenors, the contraltos and the mezzos, above all the sopranos. A fine coloratura, he maintained, was worth her weight in platinum. 'Tae *hear* her, Jamie,' he would say. 'Och, tae *hear* her; the lilt and glitter of her, swoopin' in o'er the band. The light and lovely wine of her, best ta'en young . . .' His eyes would gleam and moisten at the mere thought of such a lady. He would smother them with flowers, drink champagne from their slippers, or any of their belongings not susceptible to damage by damp. From all of which outpourings it was my habit to stand back; partly because it was no function of my situation either to criticize or acclaim, but largely because transports of delight are not a vice in which I habitually indulge. As for the ladies themselves—but I feel I have expressed their reaction adequately enough. Though to be strictly fair, it does seem possible some of them may have appreciated Ardkinross for its intrinsic merits. Certainly on a fine spring day, the pinewoods tipped with their buds of vivid green; or in the gloaming, with the heather scent coming from the hills, the tall windows of the house throwing their shafts of light across the grass, it was a bonny spot.

It has occurred to me that there may be some of you who have not heard of our establishment; which would indicate that you take no interest either in the musical stage or the internal affairs of Scotland, a state of things that I fear is only too common. There can surely be none of you though unaware of the events following the appearance among us of the personage who became known as the Diva; that would mean you have had no access to the BBC, the ITV, the *Sun* or any other of the media with which we have latterly been blessed.

I recall the night of her arrival with some clarity. I had been overseeing the planting of the beds of gillivers, the scent of which was such a feature of the early seasons at Ardkinross. At the day's end, returning to my cottage at the foot of the glen, I was much taken by the unseasonal play of lightning above the clouds. The flickerings were continuous and stretched from horizon to horizon, although as yet there was no thunder. I remember I frowned a little as I pushed open my garden gate. A gentle precipitation, of the type I have heard vulgarly described as Scotch mist, would have been entirely welcome; but a sudden storm would wash away much of the day's work. No rain fell at all however, although the display continued with unabated vigour. I took my tea and later retired to an upper room, from the windows of which the full grandeur could be better observed. The masses of vapour rolling overhead parted from time to time, affording wide glimpses of the land; the hills of Sunart and Ardnamurchan showed clear in the blazings of pink. Bolt after bolt passed hissing to the south, like the flares of the rocket devices employed to travel to such out of the way places as the moon. Between the discharges, the night seemed blacker by contrast. I was later put in mind of a fanciful notion that for a time enjoyed a considerable vogue; that the Diva in fact proceeded from deepest space, and was not of the Earth at all. Though that of course was patent nonsense; even as the supposed chariots passed, her first performance was already being given.

I smoked a pipe through, and was considering retiring for the night when the telephone from the big house tinkled. It was His Lordship. 'What d'ye mak' o' it, Jamie?' cried he in high excitement. 'The telly willna function; and there's naught on the radio but pops and heathen splutterings!'

Since I possess neither device, I was not unduly concerned. 'It would appear, sir,' I said, 'to be a species of electrical disturbance.'

He began to chuckle. 'Mon,' said he, 'does naethin' fash ye? There's Elmo's fire on a' the chumneypots, and the strangest whizzings in the sky. I tell ye, sometning's afoot!'

I observed that, unusual though these events might be, I saw no immediate cause for alarm; but he broke in once more. 'I'm no' alarmed,' he said indignantly. 'I'm no' alarmed at a'. But can ye no feel the sheer *exceetment* o' it? The verra alteration o' the air? The world is changin', mon; changin' for a' time!'

I was, if I am to be strictly truthful, more inclined to suspect an overindulgence in the excellent family brew; at such times cosmic events not infrequently took place, but always inside Willie's head. On this occasion though, he was correct.

The thunder began as I extinguished my light; a rich and velvet growling, soft at first but increasing stealthily in volume, like the percussion section of an orchestra tuning their instruments for a strange and mighty symphony. I lay and listened for a while, but there seemed no menace in it; finally, it lulled me to sleep.

I expected, from his tone of the night before, that His Lordship might be just a trifle late in rising; however he was on the step next morn, and pounding at the door before I had properly finished mashing my tea. 'Look at this, mon,' he cried, flinging a newspaper onto the table. 'And this noo, here. Have ye e'er seen the like before?'

It had been his habit for a number of years to have the major

London dailies sent up on the train, and here was a representative selection. All bore marks of hasty recomposition; and all carried headlines of vast and foreboding size. COVENT GARDEN GRINDS TO HALT, I read; and in another place, THE NIGHT OF WONDERS IN DRURY LANE. My first notion was that the Gordon riots had broken out afresh, and indeed the reports did read a little in that vein. The cause of the disturbance seemed however to have been a theatrical performance; 'Given,' as one amazed reporter observed, 'beneath a sky glowing like a scene from the London Blitz.' There were photographs of that as well; the phenomena we had experienced at Ardkinross had apparently been nothing compared to those that had visited the capital. Frightened mobs converged on the city churches; others, more opportunistically, had engaged in a major outbreak of vandalism and looting. The focus of disturbance though had been a public concert given by a young soprano called Ronda Ouspenski.

'Called whom?' I asked in some surprise. 'I do not seem to recollect the name.'

'Ye've never *haird* the name,' cried Willie exultantly. 'Nor I, nor onnybody in the whole wide world!' He riffled through more papers, flinging newsprint about the kitchen in his enthusiasm. 'Listen tae this,' he said. *'Wi' the first notes, a feeling o' peace stole o'er me the like o' whuch nae words can express. I floated in a limitless void o' space. There swum before me, flower-decked, the temples o' a' Antiquity. Frae within them, other voices breathed a promise o' ineffable sweetness. At last it was as if the verra grass was decked wi' stars; and the lion lay doon wi' the lamb, in the golden peace o' an endless afternoon . . .'*

'Merciful heavens,' said I, shocked to the core. 'Who on earth wrote that?'

'*A music critic*,' bellowed the Laird, hurling the paper on high . '*A music critic*, can ye no imagine? Were there e'er such times? I told ye the noo, a mighty change was comin'. Man, it's upon us!'

'He must have gone out of his mind,' I said. But Willie shook his head. 'They're a' like it,' he said happily. 'Each an' evra one, see f'r y'rsel'. No' a single "excessive parlando", no' a single "tonal inadequacy" in the whole carping, whining, idle, useless, self-satisfied pack! Nae "clumsy articulations", nae "fiorituri found wanting", nae "unsuitable tessituras," nae sneers, nae qualifications; nae ifs and ands and buts, nae pats o' the haid frae folk who couldna' reach the merest bootstraps o' the lassie. Man, she laid 'em by the heels; each an' evra miserable, sinning, tone-deaf, purblind herring-gutted mother's son!'

I should perhaps have mentioned that of all the passions that informed His Lordship's life, his hatred of music critics was the most ecstatic and profound.

'D'ye see what she can do?' he went on, grabbing my shoulder in a vicelike grip. 'She has the true magic on her; the ancient *weesdom*, lost this mony a year. Hear her, and ye gae tae Arcady; no' the gelatine an' cardboard thing these critic laddies tak' it for, nae a sort o' gold-roofed but an' ben, but the place *itsail*. What does it say? "Where the lion lays doon wi' the lamb". The auld place, Jamie, frae the dawn o' airth, before men foond the stain o' mortal sin. She can send ye tae Paradise!'

'Sir,' said I in my sternest tones, 'Paradise may be well enough in its way; but I remain tae be convinced that Arcady is a place in which a good Presbyterian should wish tae find himself.' He was not to be put off though. 'I must gae tae London,' cried he. 'This verra day. Ye must come too; after a', ye're my audest and staunchest help. She must sing at Ardkinross; she must and *wull*. She'll grace our hoose, Jamie, if it takes the last ha'pence oota ma purse!'

'But sir,' I said, 'how may we be sure she has even remained in the country?'

He waved a hand impatiently. 'There are sich things as telephones, mon,' he said. 'I've already made *enqueeries*. I know the verra hotel at which she's staying . . .'

There are times when gentle, reasoned argument has been known to sway Willie from a projected course of action. This, though, was not one of them. I shook my head sadly, and decided to save the breath I might otherwise have spent. Over the years I had come to know his moods indifferently well; and I realized that on this occasion he meant every last syllable.

The later editions of the newspapers, collected on the long journey south, filled in a little more detail; though who the Diva really was, and from whence she had sprung so ready-armed, was still a mystery, and was to remain so. What was clear was that the audience she had so enchanted had stubbornly refused first to quit the theatre, then to clear the road outside. Units of local police, the fire brigade and the SPG had alike failed to dislodge them; it had taken the Diva herself, singing an improvised Vocalise from the top of a fire engine, to persuade them to disperse. They went their separate ways then, reportedly with tears in their eyes and every protestation of brotherly love; and the critics staggered to their lonely cells, to pen their visions of the world beyond. I shook my head again. Willie was my employer; so if he wished my presence in London, then it behoved me to go. I confess though that I failed to see what part a gardener from Argyllshire might profitably play in such events. Doubtless it shows a certain failing in ambition; but I have always been perfectly content to have my horizon restricted by a bed of gilliflowers.

London when we reached it bore something of the aspect of a city under siege. Shopfronts were boarded over, while the streets were still littered in places with the debris of the night before. Neither was I reassured by my first sight of our destination. The street outside it was blocked from side to side by a mass of hooting traffic; a contingent of harassed-looking policemen was vainly attempting to keep the vehicles moving, but it seemed the battle was a losing one. Large Outside Broadcast vehicles drawn up on the pavement added to the congestion; beyond was the flashing blue lamp of an ambulance, caught helplessly in the crush. The lobby of the hotel itself was filled by an excited crowd that spilled out through the glass doors and across the path; it was composed, as I later discovered, of journalists, theatrical agents and impresarios in roughly equal numbers, Tempers, as I suppose was natural under the circumstances, were more than a little frayed; fists and boots were flying, papers and briefcases waved wildly in the air, while the din that arose I would be hard put to describe. 'Sir,' I said, somewhat concerned, 'it would seem we have little chance of encountering the lady in person.' But Willie was not to be deterred. 'Whisht, mon,' cried he, 'Am I no' the Laird o' Ardkinross?' He plunged into the *mêlée*, and I followed him perforce.

Several minutes of pushing and shoving barely enabled us to clear the doors. 'It is hopeless, sir,' I cried, already out of my breath; but His Lordship shook his head. 'I dinna accept the waird, Jamie,' he roared back. 'Tactics are required, mon; strategy. Follow me . . .'

To one side of the place, and pushed back now hard against the wall, tables had been set out as for a reception. Willie ducked under the cloth of the nearest; I marked his progress by the sudden violent shaking of a potted palm, heard him swear and followed once more.

At least the ploy allowed us a breathing space. We set out cautiously again, negotiating the legs of chairs, and popping our heads up from time to time to verify our bearings. 'Obsairve the tricolor eyes,' hissed the Laird, who was at the time preparing a monograph on the work of M. Rimbaud. 'Note the faces o' steel, dotted wi' gold stars; most violent paradise o' the furious grimace! Och, the Chinese, Hottentots an' fools . . .' He vanished again abruptly, bobbed up once more. 'Ah,' he cried, 'we come tae the beauteous Being, mon, tae stanch her black an' scarlet wounds . . .'

I had for once no necessity to translate the somewhat personal words; for I also had glimpsed the Diva. She sat at the head of a long table, smiling and nodding gravely, appearing quite unconcerned at the uproar round about. What she was saying was of course quite lost; but she seemed, gracefully, to be declining all blandishments. 'On,' cried Willie, waving his arm furiously. 'On, Jamie, f'r y'r *leef*!'

I was not able wholly to dismiss the notion that our mode of approach lacked something in dignity; but His Lordship had never been deterred by small considerations of that nature. Not, at least, when the good name of Ardkinross was at stake. 'Miss Ouspenski,' he hissed to her unresponding knees, 'I have a rare proposal for ye.' She moved a foot, delicately crossed her legs; but paid no other heed. 'Miss Ouspenski,' cried Willie again in mounting passion; he is not a man accustomed to being ignored. 'I wish tae discuss a *business proposition*!' She shifted her position once more, but otherwise still paid no attention; and Willie, beside himself with rage, did something no Laird, or commoner for that, should ever do. He actually reached out, in an attempt to grip her ankle. His hand closed on naught but air; he looked baffled for a moment, then began to laugh. 'D'ye see the *claverness*, Jamie?' he cried in delight. 'D'ye see the *skill*? T'is a holographic *deveece*; we are being tested . . .' He leaped from beneath the table, passed clear through the image of the Diva, roared '*Chruachan*' in his most daunting voice and charged for the double doors beyond.

My attempt to emulate him met with somewhat qualified success; I caught my foot, and incontinently measured my length. I sat up somewhat winded; but one glimpse of the charging mob behind me had me on my feet again. I was through the doors and had slammed them before, I suppose, I had had much opportunity for reflection. I landed on hands and knees, and looked around me.

The first objects of which I actually became aware were His Lordship's feet, which were dangling roughly on a level with my face. He was in the grip of a foreign-looking young gentleman of considerable stature who had raised him one-handed by the lapels of his jacket and was regarding him with a far from friendly gaze. The face of the aggressor was swarthy, with thick, dark brows that met in a single line above his deepset eyes. He was dressed in a uniform of white leather, set off by black and highly polished topboots. His mouth was a little open, and from it proceeded a somewhat alarming sound; a species of purring growl from which I concluded, rightly as it transpired, that the poor fellow was bereft of ordinary speech. His other physical abilities, however, were patently unimpaired; Willie's face was turning from red to purplish black, and he was emitting faint noises not inconsistent with the notion of strangulation. I rose cautiously, and was considering my best method of approach when a light and silvery voice said, 'Put him down please, Lorenzo; I'm sure he means no harm.' The giant grunted in a disappointed sort of way and dropped the Laird contemptuously, rather like an old and unwanted sack. 'I stooped over him, attempting to loosen his tie, but Willie pushed me impatiently away. I followed the direction of his gaze, and saw the Diva.

My reactions, I suppose, were mixed to say the least. Certainly she was far from being the goddess-like figure my imagination, that general curse of mankind, had already partially constructed. She was in fact somewhat on the short side, no more than five feet one or two, and definitely inclined, though it may perhaps be ungallant of me to say so, to stockiness. There was too in her manner a certain stolid placidity; though that also, in time, ceased to surprise me. Certainly she had no very clear idea of the effect her voice could have, nor did she ever seem particularly concerned; in general she viewed the scenes of turmoil that customarily surrounded her with a species of faint puzzlement, as if they could have no connection with her but were expressions merely of general human illogic. Nor could she ever be induced to discuss her art, beyond the somewhat lukewarm observation that she found that singing relaxed her; she was in short the agent of a force, with no notion of what that force might be, or from whence it emanated. She sat at a little table, contentedly munching grapes, and watched us with what I can only describe as amused docility.

The Laird, still on the carpet, had already begun his speech. 'Diva,' he cried, 'incomparable one. I come tae offer ye the freedom of ma hoose; the finest in the land, built for ye, conceived for ye, waiting for ye, incomplete withoot ye. And tae beg, on ma ane twa knees, that ye'll condescend tae grace it wi' y'r presence . . .'

The Diva selected another grape. 'You must be Lord Ardkinross then,' she said amiably. 'All right, I'll come. They say it's rather nice up there; you'd like it, wouldn't you, Lorenzo?'

Willie jumped to his feet. 'Is it possible?' he cried. 'Madam, ye do me too much honour . . .' He sprang forward to take her hand, and would have kissed it; but a bloodcurdling growl from Lorenzo stopped him in his tracks. 'I wouldn't do that,' said the Diva, sounding a little disappointed. 'He really doesn't care for it, you know.'

A thunderous knocking began, on the doors behind us; but the Laird ignored it. He was already delving into his pockets; he produced crackling sheets of paper, which he proceeded to unfold and lay out on the table. 'I have here,' he cried, 'ma standard form o' *contract*. Ye'll obsairve, Ma'am, that the critical line of a' is left a blank, for ye tae fill in as ye choose . . .' But the Diva waved a hand, looking faintly alarmed. 'Oh, no,' she said, 'I never do things like that. I've said I'll come, and so I will.' She looked thoughtful. 'I'll come,' she said, 'a year and a day from now. I have some things to do first . . .' And with that, His Lordship had to rest content.

We made our way from the place by means of a fire escape, shown to us by the ever-obliging Lorenzo; throughout our journey home Willie babbled unceasingly, still unable, it seemed, to credit his good fortune. 'A year an' a day, Jamie,' he cried. 'A year an' a day, ye have the *note* o' it . . .' He shook his head. 'It gives us precious little *teem*,' he said, 'but it wull have tae serve. Ardkinross must be redecorated, frae top tae toe; also, there wull be flowers. The finest display in a' the land, that's what I'll be wantin' frae ye. Roses sairtainly, an' *lullies*; plus onything else ye care tae choose. I'm in y'r hands, mon, and I'll trust y'r judgement. Ye may turn o'er the big greenhoose tae their propagation; plus onything else ye may require.' He clapped me on the back. 'It wull be the event,' he proclaimed, 'of a *leefteem* . . .' Which was one sentiment with which I could at least heartily concur.

As I feared, he was as good as his word; preparations for the great day were put in hand directly, commencing with the widening and resurfacing of the road to Ardkinross, a project for which the Laird had frequently been petitioned but which he had as frequently brushed aside. He confided to me an intention to line it with triumphal arches, which evidences of earthly pomp he would also require to be wreathed with floral tributes; a project which mercifully came to naught. There were limits it would seem, even to the fortunes of the House of Ardkinross. His other improvements went forward rapidly enough though. The formal terraces surrounding the house were refurbished, and new turf laid; masons were engaged to replace those of the balusters decayed beyond repair and stone urns of portentous size appeared, the addition of which to my eyes did little to improve the vista. All of which I suffered with what dignity I could command; my limit of forbearance was however reached with the arrival of a species of statue the like of which I had certainly never beheld, at least at Ardkinross. I hied myself at once to the Laird, who in typical fashion sought to brush away my complaint. 'Whisht, mon,' said he, 'ye have nae consideration in the matter o' *Airt*. Yon's Diana the Chaste Huntress, great Goddess o' a' the Auncients . . .' I was not however to be mollified. 'Sir,' said I, 'the lady's private life is nae concern o' mine. For all I ken, what ye say may well be right; but I willna

have a brazen lassie such as yon vaunt hersel' o'er my proper
place o' wairk . . .'

His Lordship chewed his lip, and looked as angry as I had
ever seen him. 'I willna be dictated to in ma ain hoose,' cried he,
'not by ony leevin' mon . . .' Then, unexpectedly, he brightened.
'Whisht, Jamie,' said he again, 'but we forget oursel's. Come,
tak' a dram. I canna dispense with ye; and she's but a *treefle*,
after a'. A' is for the One who is tae come . . .' He began to
laugh. 'She can gae tae the vegetable garden,' he said, 'where I
can see her frae ma study window. T'is an ill wind indeed, that
blaes nae guid at a' . . .'

'Then,' said I, 'Hamish may tak' charge o' the area, a process
he wull nae doot enjoy.' Which last was certainly true; indeed
the young heathen later went so far as to swear the new addition
had had a positive effect upon the produce. Never, in living
memory, had we grown such vegetable marrows.

While we thus occupied ourselves, the Diva's meteoric career
of course continued. She sang, in that first and only season, in
every major opera house in the world; in between such engage-
ments, and by way presumably of relaxation, she attended each
and every music festival, from Edinburgh to Spoleto. Everywhere
in her wake, new understandings blossomed; old scores were left
unsettled, old battles unresolved. Presidents of international
companies smilingly disgorged decades of unpaid tax; an entire
family of Mafiosi tearfully turned itself over to the Federal
government, who released them with the mildest of admonitions,
since they were patently incapable of further public harm.
Promoters mounted concerts at their own expense, for love of
their fellow men; critics sang their noble paeans of praise,
journalists penned warm and gentle prose. Their editors raged;
till one by one they themselves also attended recitals, and fell
beneath the spell. After which their leader articles became alike
suffused with a calm and golden glow. They had, each one of
them, heard the pipes of Arcady.

Often, at the end of the day's work, the Laird would call me
to the house to partake of a little refreshment; and so I saw many
of the Diva's exploits for myself, on the large coloured television
set that dominated His Lordship's private lounge. She was
frequently interviewed, though the results were invariably the

same. She appeared, if anything, even less communicative than on our own first meeting. She would smile, in the polite, stolid way she had, and say that she was pleased folk liked her work; while Lorenzo, her chauffeur and private aide, hovered in the background, scowling round him in the lights and cameras, grunting and hissing to express his broad approval, or the lack thereof. He too, it seemed, was increasingly a force to be reckoned with; he was frequently pictured at the wheel of the Rolls-Royce Phantom motor car in which he drove her, that had been a gift from an anonymous admirer and to the dashboard of which he had attached a Schmeisser sub-machine gun, ostensibly for the discouragement of such minor and as yet unconverted elements as traffic wardens. His loyalty to his mistress was beyond praise; though it did lead on occasions to confrontations that could only be described as unfortunate. In the course of one of them he apparently hurled a somewhat too importunate young journalist over a garden wall. The garden, it transpired, was on the roof of a skyscraper in Manhattan; and Lorenzo would undoubtedly have suffered at the very least a period of incarceration had not the Diva undertaken to sing at his defence. He was released at once and later pictured unrepentantly waving his machine-gun, after which a delighted press dubbed him 'The Magnificent.'

Miss Ouspenski, it seemed, put herself to considerable trouble in the matter, with the inevitable result that the personal relationship of the couple was called into prurient question. Base slanders were insinuated by the less responsible of the world's journalists; or by those at least who as yet had not felt the full force of the Diva's charm. This last category of persons was still relatively numerous; for it was rapidly established that however the magic was wrought, her personal presence was an essential ingredient. Recordings of her voice were of course made in plenty, but all attempts to reproduce its unique effect failed. And energetic though her programme was—it was a matter of continuing wonderment to many, not least the Laird, how flesh and blood could sustain such a hectic pace at all—she could not, in the nature of things, be everywhere at once. Willie was in fact heard to mutter on more than one occasion that she would burn herself out completely before ever reaching Ardkinross; the thought tended to throw him into the deepest of depressions. However as the year passed with no detectable flagging of her energies, his spirits once more revived. 'Think on it, Jamie,' he would say; 'just think on it, mon. In a few short months, she wull be here; I shall hear her at last, under ma ain roof, and *leef* wull be complete!' One evening indeed he ran to the Great Hall, flung back the doors that gave onto the auditorium, the dark and waiting stage. 'Look, mon,' he breathed. 'Wull ye no *regard* it?'

I stood beside him dutifully, observing the tall, still drapes that rose to shadow, the tiers on tiers of seats; the graceful lines of windows, their curtains parted to the blueing dusk. The air of the place struck cool; and there was the faint, ever-present scent of polish and dust. Somewhere a solitary bird was piping, but all else was still. I made to speak, but His Lordship gripped my arm. 'Hush,' he said. 'Hush a wee. Can ye no *feel* it? The quiet, like the centre o' the univairse? Can ye no feel it's *waitin'* for her? And can ye no sense *them*? She's a' o' them, Jamie; a' the singers, right on through the ages, a' the little lassies who burned an' sparked like rockets, only tae fall back. Tae dust, an' tae forgetfulness.' He sighed. 'We shall ne'er see her like again,' he said. 'The rest is shadows . . .'

I did not answer. There seemed nothing to be said; though if a rejoinder had occurred to me, I feel that I would still have held my peace. I was after all in a slightly embarrassed situation; it was not the first time I had suspected His Lordship of harbouring curious notions, but this was downright unorthodoxy. For a time I almost found it within myself to wish that for all our sakes, but foremost for the sake of the Laird, the Diva would not in fact honour the obligation into which she had entered so freely. A part of me knew though, with a curious certainty, that she would indeed present herself on schedule. Had I also understood that her first performance at Ardkinross would be her last on earth, I wonder what my feelings might then have been.

Gifts continued to shower on her; she became, will-he, nill-he, the mistress of properties as far removed each from the next as a Texan ranch house and a mediaeval Spanish castle. All of which she accepted with a species of calm gravity, as though they were after all no more than her due; yet overall it seemed possessions

meant very little to her. Certainly at no time did she put herself
to trouble in their acquisition; rather it was as if they simply
collected round her, as her great motor car had arrived from the
blue one day and as indeed had Lorenzo, who it transpired had
simply presented himself on her doorstep one bright morning
and had indicated, by his uniquely personal range of gestures,
that he wished nothing from life other than to serve her. He
alone, I suspected, she valued highly; a fact which subsequent
events were to prove correct.

The year turned, finally; and the Diva announced through the
medium of Reuters, by now virtually her private press agency,
that she considered her first world tour to be complete. It was
generally supposed that she would allow herself a holiday, and
Willie for one heaved a monstrous sigh of relief. She did drop
out of sight certainly, to rest up at one or another of her retreats;
but the break was of short duration. Certain Arab potentates had
expressed an interest in observing at close hand what was to
them a uniquely European phenomenon, and had invited her to
tour their countries; within a week she had popped up again,
still accompanied by the faithful Lorenzo, this time in the Middle
East. What followed surpassed all expectations. She sang not for
the private delectation of her hosts but in guerrilla strongholds,
refugee camps and oil refineries. Anywhere, in fact, in which she
found herself; and once again she left a trail of consternation.
Her talents, it seemed, were strictly non-denominational. Phalan-
gists tore the icons from their gunshields, replacing them with
images of the new goddess; Copts embraced Muslims, Turks
were seen to kiss Greeks, Syrians fell weeping on the necks of
their brothers of Zion. The most entrenched of combatants
retreated to their separate heavens; and one by one the guns fell
silent. A peace descended such as that troubled quarter of the
globe had not known for centuries.

The media by now had given up any serious attempt to cover
other world events. Even the so-called conquest of space, once
dubbed by many the greatest of mankind's adventures and a
project in which our species was currently feverishly involved,
paled into insignificance and was largely relegated to the back
pages of the dailies. The relief of the Martian colony, which
since the failure of its hydroponics plant had been suffering

steady starvation, passed virtually unremarked; the establishment of the first scheduled service between Earth and the moon was greeted by little more than sniffs, while the colonisation of the satellites of Jupiter no doubt went forward smoothly enough but rated scarcely more than the odd remark. All paled before the exploits of the Diva; folk asked themselves, with many a puzzled scratching of the head, where she might next be expected to turn her attention, and what the result would be. The answer was not long in coming. A large transport aircraft was either hired or lent for the occasion, the Rolls-Royce trundled aboard; and she and Lorenzo set off for South America.

By the time of her return some six weeks later, roughly a third of the known world was at peace; and likely to remain so, since none of those so far converted had shown any tendency toward apostasy. Interviewed at London Airport by a thousand or so journalists, she remarked somewhat predictably that she was glad folk continued to enjoy her singing, and that it was probably a good thing if for the time being at least they desisted from blowing each other to fragments. These sterling sentiments were received with jubilant acclaim. Only Lorenzo, scowling about him with his finger on the trigger of the Schmeisser, seemed less than wholly content with the new order; and it came to me, I suppose a trifle belatedly, that this was only to be expected. After all, the poor soul had never heard, nor could ever hear, a single note that she sang.

The date of her promised appearance at Ardkinross was by now less than a week away; and His Lordship, having spent considerable sums on advertising the event and having moreover booked the theatre to several times its actual capacity in the pious hope that the Diva could be persuaded to extend her stay, was understandably a trifle on edge. The uncertainties were however resolved by the arrival next morning of a telegram affirming that she would indeed be with us on the twentieth of the month, assuring us that she was very much looking forward to the visit and adding, a trifle obscurely I felt, that Lorenzo sent his love. It galvanized the Laird into fresh activity. Representatives of a catering firm arrived, to discuss arrangements for the buffet supper he had also advertised; a burly, whiskered fellow clad in a spectacular tartan—to which I doubt he had the right—

negotiated at length the terms for the pipe band that had been
laid on, while the last to make his appearance was a nervous-
looking keeper from the local safari park. He was in charge of a
crated and somewhat irritable peacock, the duties of which would
be to strut the terracing, greeting the guests with appropriate
dignity and spectacle. As things transpired, the creature did not
in fact survive to the day of the great event. Its sole talent proved
to be a skill in ambush that would have aroused the admiration
of the great Rob Roy himself; its chief delight was to secrete
itself in the shrubbery, from whence it would hurtle with bloodcurdling shrieks at the heads of any unfortunate enough to pass
its hiding place. It received its quietus not from the classic
bodkin but via a mattock wielded by Hamish MacDougall; the
lad has always been remarkably sharp on his feet. While in the
main I deplore physical violence, I must admit to feeling little
grief; seldom have I encountered a more maladjusted bird.

The longed-for morning dawned at last. Willie, who had
been up and about since before first light, fumed and fretted
throughout the entire day, dashing from point to point to
supervise the placement of stage draperies, the setting up of
lights and the siting of bouquets; ordering this, countermanding
that and generally making of himself an ineffable pest. All were
relieved when shortly after six o'clock the first of the scouts he
had stationed about the terrain reported that the cavalcade was
finally in sight. And in truth it was a remarkable spectacle.
First came the police motor-bicyclists who had latterly found it
necessary to escort the Diva in most of her journeyings; then the
Laird's own Bentley, despatched to Fort William to guide the
convoy home. Pennants flew from its wings; its chrome and
coachwork gleamed immaculate. Next came the pipers, their
bright plaids swinging, their instruments skirling out a march.
Finally came the Diva herself, in her great white whispering
carriage. Even Lorenzo, it seemed, had caught in part at least
the festive air; his habitual somewhat sinister attire had been
discarded for a uniform of pale blue linen, replete with epaulettes
and golden froggings, though as ever his eyes gleamed suspiciously behind his large sunglasses. The only dissonant note
was in fact provided by his mistress. To ward off, presumably,
the early evening air she had erected above herself a large and

rather shabby black umbrella, beneath which she sat contentedly, waving a hand from time to time like some latterday Victoria. Behind her came the first of a cavalcade of vehicles; the audience, or rather several audiences, each member of which seemed determined that his ticket, and his alone, entitled him to view the first performance. They spilled across the grass, abandoning their vehicles anywhere and everywhere despite the efforts of the staff; and the grounds, on which so much care had been lavished during the last twelve months, began to assume the appearance of a shambles. Before the Diva had properly alighted, an incipient riot was well under way.

Willie, wreathed in the smiles to which I suppose he was entitled and the full regalia of a clan chieftain, to which he most certainly was not, met his guest at the house steps and whisked her away, afterwards returning to harangue the increasingly angry mob. As ever, his golden oratory won the day; although it did take a burst from Lorenzo's ever-ready Schmeisser fully to engage their attention. Pink ticketholders, it was decided, would hear the first part of the recital; blue the second, and green the third. The performance to begin at eight sharp; the buffet and licensed bars to be opened at once. A fragile peace was thus restored; but the alarms of the day were very far from over. The first of the ticket holders were in their places, and the curtain about to be rung up, when distant shouts announced the arrival of a further force. It hove in sight between the rhododendron beds, came tramping along the drive; it resolved itself into most of the population of the village, waving placards of portentous size and led by the Reverend MacAllister, a preacher of the good old school and tireless in the prosecution of his faith. The notices proclaimed the sinfulness of singing, dancing, musicmaking and almost anything else one cared to mention, but above all of listening to the Diva; a Scarlet Woman apparently, come to steal away the hapless souls of men. The police, reinforced in expectation of some such turn of events, ran to head the marchers off; but to no avail. The procession surged relentlessly forward, colliding first with a section of the still-potential audience then with the pipe band itself, which on certain promises, mainly concerned with the well-stocked cellars of Ardkinross, had undertaken the further defence of life, limb and property. A score of separate scuffles broke out at once; but the main body of invaders, drilled apparently with military precision, pressed forward to the terraces, where they collected in an angry mob, stamping, shouting and showing every sign of storming the place itself. The Diva, however, was unconcerned. 'Please let them come in,' she said. 'I'm sure they only want to stand at the back.' So the doors were flung open, later the windows too; her first notes floated out, and a breathing calm descended.

I watched with a species of astonishment. At first there was little change to be remarked, save that the restlessness of the folk within the hall was wholly stilled, replaced by that hush of concentration that is the peculiar magic, and occasionally the glory, of the stage. Then it was as if a light began to dawn, spreading from face to face. Men and women alike seemed wholly transfigured; some wept as openly as children, others turned unconsciously to grip their neighbours' hands. A dozen burly bandsmen, still poised to battle the insurgents, froze in blank amazement; beside me the Reverend MacAllister, tears coursing down his cheeks, fell to his knees and raised his arms to heaven, a mortification, certainly, to which his noble spirit had hitherto been unsubjected. It was as if invisible strings attached them one and all to the Diva. Her mouth popped open and closed, her hands jerked regularly, themselves like the limbs of a puppet; and insensibly the folk around me began to fade. A golden glow seemed stealing through the very walls; then Ardkinross itself was shrinking, to a mote against a broad and pearly plain. It seemed I hung outside it, watching down; till I quickly pressed my fingers to my ears, firming the wads of cotton wool that I had placed there. The unwanted visions retreated; the Diva became once more a short and somewhat unimpressive figure, gesturing woodenly from the little stage.

I met His Lordship during the first recess. The Laird was walking rather like a man in a dream, though he jerked to attention rapidly enough when he saw me. He stared and pointed, his mouth working violently; and though I cannot exactly say I *heard* the words, I had little difficulty in construing their import. 'Mon,' he bellowed, 'what are ye thinkin' of? Why hae ye stopped y'r ears?'

I drew myself up. 'Sir,' I said, 'ye must understand my

poseetion. My Grandfather was a founder member o' the Wee Frees . . .' Which is, I fancy, a matter of common knowledge; besides which, I have my own standards to maintain. And I will do that in the manner I deem most fitting, though I have never been one for marching about with banners.

After that, there was no more thought of intervals. The Diva sang and sang, holding her audience, and those others who crowded round the doors, in the effortless cup of her hands. What visions passed before their eyes, I have no means of knowing; nor, I suppose, will any of them ever tell. Neither have I a notion of how long the performance went on, save that by the time it ended, dusk had turned to night; and the Diva stepped back finally, smiling and bowing, the curtain gently fell.

The scenes that I had witnessed were remarkable enough; but they were nothing to what followed. The storm of clapping, cheering and stamping that broke out penetrated even my defences, and seemed fit to bring the roof in. Over it, faintly, came a fusillade of shots as Lorenzo discharged the Schmeisser at the ceiling, apparently his customary method of signifying approval. 'Though at least,' as the Laird later philosophically remarked, 'he showed a mite o' *tact*. It was nae on *automatic* . . .'

The Diva was recalled again and again, till it seemed the encores might go on as long as the concert itself. Finally though, as I realized by the growing awareness in the faces that surrounded me, she began the great *Vocalise* with which she woke an audience from its trance. Softer and gentler grew her gestures, while her voice dropped, as I was later told, to a mere thread of sound. The charm was all but wound up.

Having retained what passes for my wits, I had been keeping a keen lookout around me. Had I not been thus engaged I doubt if I would have remarked the rather bland-faced young man in the centre front row at all. As things were, there was little enough of note about him; save that he gripped some object firmly in his palm, and that his ears, like mine, were blocked with cotton wool. The circumstance seemed curious to say the least; and I was edging forward, intent on some enquiry, when the song at last ended. The Diva stood head bowed, her hands at her sides; and there was a breathless moment before the final curtainfall. In it the young man rose unhurriedly, raising his arm. The object he gripped, I saw, was a hand grenade. He removed the pin, held it the appropriate few seconds and lobbed it accurately to the performer's feet.

'*Get doon*,' I roared in horror. I ran toward the stage; but the gesture was a futile one. I had no chance of reaching the thing in time, and knew it perfectly well.

There was one, though, who was quicker. Lorenzo, moving for all his bulk like a streak of well-greased lightning, pounded from the wings. One great arm hurled the Diva back; then he had flung himself face down across the device. Never did he more deserve his title of Magnificent; next instant, the term had ceased to apply.

The concussion, and the fearful roar, half stunned me; I staggered about, my hands to my face, sensing the panic as the audience took to its heels and still disjointedly glad of the protection with which I had seen fit to equip myself. When I could see again the Laird, ashen-faced, held the Diva in his arms, while on the stagefront lay—but I do not feel I need attempt too detailed a description. The imagination of the reader will, I fancy, fill in the details readily enough.

The first of the helicopters landed a matter of minutes later, swooping in over the packed and panicking cars. Others followed, till the grounds somewhat resembled the aftermath of an air show. I walked away, sat wearily in the rear stalls and waited for the visitors to arrive. The first to step into the hall, as I had half expected, was the President of the United States. He was followed by the Prime Minister of Britain, several assorted Sheikhs and some half dozen others whose faces, I am sure, would be familiar to you if you are in any sense a follower of current affairs.

The President stared round him at the carnage with a somewhat weary air. Then he walked forward to the stage, placed his hands on his hips and stood looking down. He regarded the shivering Diva; finally he spoke. The words, I feel sure, should be inscribed somewhere in letters of gold; but perhaps they already are. 'Wal,' he said, 'guess we screwed up agin . . .'

I suppose it was an hour or more before things had quietened down. By that time Ardkinross was sealed off by the appropriate ring of security men; an emergency communications room had been hastily set up and the Diva, the Laird and myself sat with the visitors in Willie's spacious lounge. The President swilled Bourbon round in his glass, drank thoughtfully and produced a lean black cigar. One of his half dozen lounge-suited bodyguards leaned down to light it for him. He blew smoke, and beamed at the Diva benignly. 'Y'see, little lady,' he said, 'it goes like so. We tried for the quiet solootion; but like uh said, we goofed. Maybe yuh'll hold that agin us, and uh cain't say I'd blame yuh; but uh surely hope yuh won't. 'Cos we gotta come out in the open, talk a little turkey.'

The Diva did not answer.

'Yuh see,' went on the President, 'yuh just don't seem t' grasp the inconveenience yuh bin causin' round this li'l ol' globe. Why, we even had us a summit conference all 'bout it, right here in li'l ol' London; but we ain't come up with no answer.'

The Diva sat with her eyes downcast, and her hands gripped in her lap. 'I didn't want to cause any trouble,' she said indistinctly. 'I didn't think I was doing.'

'That's just the point,' said the Prime Minister magisterially. 'People like you never do think. You go rushing about, poking your fingers into things that don't concern you; and you never think at all . . .'

'World economics,' said a small man in a gold-encrusted headdress, 'are a most complex matter. Oh indeed, yes . . .'

'Shame has been brought to my country,' broke in another, fiddling angrily with a large, curved dagger. 'Daily, uncircumcised dogs invade its borders. All they do is kiss my people, and profess love. It is not the will of Allah . . .'

'I am fearing lest you invade my land also,' cried a small, agitated Indian. 'I am not daring to contemplate the results. Pakis lying down with Brahmans, so many sacred cows perforated full of holes; chaos, missy, chaos! Oh, dearie, dearie me . . .'

'Be that as it may,' trumpeted the Prime Minister, holding up a hand. 'Religious tolerance, as you all well know, has long been the watchword of my Administration . . .'

'Religious, shoot,' cried the President. 'Uh ain't never lynched a nigger yait. Fact is, we'd gotten ourselves some mighty big deals goin'; an' they all fell right on through . . .'

'Do you have the faintest notion,' said the Prime Minister coldly, 'of the value in real terms of our arms trade to our brothers in the Middle East? Arms that now lie useless and rusting?'

'But nobody's *fighting* any more,' cried the Diva a little desperately. 'So they don't *need* them . . .'

'Security,' carolled the Prime Minister, 'is the only key to a true and lasting peace. Just settlements proceed from strength, and strength alone . . .'

'Yuh see, little lady,' said the President, 'the world jest plumb ain't ready.' He waved an arm, expansively. 'Out there though,' he cried, 'is a whole big Yewniverse, ripe for the pickin'.' He stubbed the cigar, leaning forward impressively. 'What we're gonna ask of yuh,' he said, 'is pretty big. But yuh strike me as a pretty big sort o' little girl. We're gonna ask yuh t'be our ambassador . . .'

Willie had been sitting somewhat owlishly, a glass in his hand, blinking from one to another of the speakers; it was he, however, who first realized the import of the words. '*No*,' he bellowed, springing up. '*No* . . . I willna hae' it . . . get oot o' ma hoose, the pack of ye. Y're naught but bliddy heathen . . .'

'Sir,' cried the President, stung, 'Have the goodness tuh keep outa muh business dealin's . . .'

'Business?' cried His Lordship. '*Business*? I'll show ye business. Some business o' ma ain . . .' It was then that I first understood that the curious effect wrought by the Diva's performance could, given sufficient stimulus, be reversed. With a wild shout, Willie ran from the room. He was back in an instant, bearing a claymore snatched from the great stand of arms in the passage beyond. 'Chruachan,' he roared, for the last time. '*Ardkinross for aye* . . .' He whirled the weapon, raised it on high and charged, empurpled, at the President of the United States.

What followed was I suppose predictable. The company had started to its feet; but the bodyguards moved fastest of all. The first stepped back, the second thrust out his leg. Willie measured his length among the fireirons, with a vast and complicated crash and an even vaster oath. The claymore flew from his hand to bury itself, wagging majestically, in the far wall; the third bodyguard tapped him above the ear with a pistol butt in an admonitory sort of way while the fourth, fifth and sixth turned him over and sat on him, all in the same practised, fluid movement. A silence descended once more, broken only by the Laird's stertorous and still-furious breathing.

The President, who I realized was the only person in the room not to have stirred a muscle, shook his head sorrowfully and drained the remainder of the Bourbon. 'Now, ah jest call that plain *stoopid*,' he said. 'Son, yuh know what yuh done? Yuh pissed on muh white flag . . .' He glanced round him. 'Yuh all agreed?'

The Sheikhs nodded stonily; but it was the United Kingdom representative who spoke. 'In twenty four hours' time,' said the Prime Minister coldly, 'the first of the Saturn vehicles will be leaving from Cape Canaveral. You will be aboard it, Madam. Her Majesty's Government will undertake to defray the costs of your removal to Florida . . .' His Lordship began to bellow again; but the Diva quietened him. 'It's all right,' she said sadly. 'I'll go; I don't mind, honestly. After all, there's nothing much to stop for any more.' She stared at the President. 'I suppose you'll want me to come at once,' she said. 'But I don't have very much packing to do.' She turned to Willie. 'You'd better keep my motor car,' she said. 'I shan't need it where I'm going. I couldn't give it back anyway, because I don't know who it belonged to. And will you . . . see to Lorenzo, please? He wouldn't mind staying here; it's nice and peaceful.' The President rose; she took his arm, turned back a final time. My heart went out to the lassie then; for her face was one great sheen of tears.

The launch, of course, was well enough publicised; pictures of the event were widely distributed by satellite, and for once the world attended. I watched with His Lordship, in the room that had recently been the scene of so much activity. My mind was still a curious mixture of emotions; while what the Laird was thinking, surely no man could say. He held his peace though, while the gantry was wheeled into position beside the mighty rocket; but when the dumpy, silver-suited figure of the Diva trudged to the entry port and turned once more to wave, he gave a groan that seemed fetched from his very boots. 'Jamie,' he cried, 'the world o' song is dead. Ardkinross is nae mair . . .' I would perhaps have offered some words of solace; but the rest was drowned, in the roaring of the rocket.

The Saturn device, as I later read, was the largest and most powerful vehicle ever to be launched from Earth; so its total disintegration, somewhere in the upper reaches of what I believe is termed the ionosphere, was correspondingly the most spectacular explosion ever to take place in space. The shockwave thus generated seemed likewise possessed of a will of its own; certainly it defied all of what till then had been assumed to be the laws of physics. It circled the earth, zigzagging in a thoroughly reprehensible fashion, and it was a full twenty four hours before its first effects were felt. His Lordship telephoned the cottage then, in a state of high excitement. 'Jamie,' he cried, 'have ye no' heard? The roof is off the Covent Garden Opera . . . !'

Other news flashes came in thick and fast. The curious structure overlooking Sydney Harbour, that I have heard described by the irreverent as the 'Nuns' Scrum', was the next to suffer; after which the wave rushed on to Italy. La Scala was reported by eyewitnesses to rise to a height of several hundred metres before dissolution inevitably set in; fortunately the place was unoccupied at the time. The Paris Opera and the little Cardiff theatre suffered similar fates, though of that the Laird professed himself unconcerned. The French, he avowed, could 'ne'er keep in *teem* onyway,' while he had never forgiven the Welsh for discovering the melodiousness of *Billy Budd*.

From Wales the effect abruptly leaped the Atlantic, to try conclusions with the New York Met. There followed a brief respite, though there was no doubt in my mind that the lull was more apparent than real. It had not escaped my notice that the incidents were taking place in a strict and unvarying sequence that corresponded exactly with the Diva's own world tour; and after all it takes more time for news to filter back from South America. I attempted to communicate the notion to the Laird; he was however wholly unimpressed. Nor did he seem willing to draw the somewhat obvious conclusion, or accept the parlousness of his present situation. 'Sir,' I urged, 'ye would be well advised to come down to the cottage for a wee while.' However he once more interrupted me. 'Whisht, mon,' he cried, 'what are ye blatherin' aboot? T'is a night o' nights. This'll teach 'em; the whole mangy pack o' 'em. T'is revenge, Jamie, a proper and just revenge; and och, t'is a sweet commodity!'

There was a sudden darkening of the air. I looked up. Clouds were massing, over the head of the glen; such clouds as I had ne'er beheld. Blue-black they were and towering as I watched, writhing from the elemental force within them. A shadow raced forward; instantly the land was dark as midnight. In the sudden gloom, I heard the first low moaning of a wind. 'My Lord,' said I urgently, 'ye havna' but a minute . . .'

'Awa' wi' ye, mon,' said he dismissively. 'T's nobbut a wee *breeze*. Think ye that a'll be driven frae ma *hoose*?'

'Willie,' I cried in desperation, 'get ooot o' there . . .'

'Watch y'r tongue, Jamie,' snapped he, sharp on the instant. 'Hae a mind tae whom ye speak. I'll no hae *over-familiarity* . . .'

'Awa', ye sassenach,' cried I. 'I dinna mind ye at a'. Ye're a pathetic wee mon. As a promoter ye'd mak' an excellent bricklayer; ye canna even brew a decent *whusky* . . .' Which last of course was inspirational on my part. To call the Laird a Lowlander was bad enough; but to intimate to any man, whether his job be the governance of nations or the sweeping of the roads, that he kens not how to do it, is the surest way to rage. The telephone gave out a series of sounds that would be difficult to describe, but that certainly seemed to emanate from no human throat. Finally His Lordship recovered, to a degree at least, the power of speech. 'By a' the gods, MacLachlan,' quoth he, 'this time ye've gane tae far. Guard y'rsel' . . .' The telephone went dead; and within a gratifyingly brief period I saw the headlights of a motor vehicle careering down the glen.

I had taken the minor precaution of slipping the bolts on the cottage door; it availed me little though. His Lordship's furious shouts were succeeded by a series of bone-jarring crashes. The stout wood splintered and swung inward, and Willie was revealed. His hair and moustaches bristled, like the hair of one of the more legendary of the Irish heroes; his eyes started; and he gripped a massive battleaxe that once, or so the family legend would have it, had been wielded by the great MacGregor himself.

Having achieved my primary object of removing him from what I deemed to be the place of danger, I would have attempted some placatory words; but he was clearly not in a reasoning vein. I jumped back; and his first blow split the table clean in twain. His second reduced a stout dresser to a condition somewhat resembling matchwood, while his third smashed the lamp, which in its way was fortunate. Burning oil ran liberally about; and he dropped the weapon at once. 'Get a sack or something, mon,' he bellowed. 'Wull ye stand an' watch ma property burn doon?'

The next few moments were decidedly fraught; but the flames were finally extinguished, to be succeeded by clouds of choking smoke. We staggered to the door; the wind howled round us, snatching at our clothes; and from the now-invisible head of the glen came a crack, followed by a dismal and protracted roar. The Laird, frozen to the spot by shock, turned to me a pale and stricken face; and I nodded sadly. 'That will be Ardkinross,' I said, 'awa' the noo . . .' A shockwave slapped at the cottage, boomed off into distance and was gone. Silence fell; the clouds swirled back as quickly as they had come, and in the still-gloomy sky burned clusterings of stars.

Willie seemed to wrestle with some strong emotion. Contrasting expressions flickered across his face; finally he turned to grip my hand. 'Jamie,' said he, 'ye auld dog. I ken y'r drift at last. Ye saved ma *leef*; and ye'll find I'm no' *ungreetful* . . .'

'Whisht,' said I. 'Look at the sky . . .'

I am not, in the main, a great respecter of miracles; at best, they always seem to have a Popish ring. On this occasion though I can only report what I observed. The stars were moving; uncertainly at first, circling round each other like a swarm of distant fireflies. Soon though they coalesced into a pattern. Their soft light glowingly joined; and the great calm face of the Diva watched down from the highest vault of heaven, bestowed on us what I can only describe as a broad, slow wink.

The Laird was on his knees, his arms outstretched. 'Great one,' he cried beseechingly, 'dinna gae awa' . . .' It was too late though; her image was fading already, to be replaced by another. Its outlines were uncertain at first; then I recognized, with shock and some foreboding, the lineaments of the great Lorenzo himself. He too smirked, in a somewhat unbecoming way; bent his right arm and mimed, with considerable exaggeration, the flexing of the muscle. He smirked once more, and slowly began to turn.

'No, mon, no,' I roared. 'Remember y'r *dignity* . . .' The plea, however, was to no avail. He already stood sideways-on; and I recoiled, covering my eyes. 'Ithyphallic' is a word that I detest, in principle and practice; but it is the only one that will serve. Then, mercifully, he too was gone; and the evening was as it had been before.

The Laird, of course, would have dashed back up the glen to view the remnants of his house; it was with difficulty that I persuaded him that such a venture would be not only foolhardy but dangerous, and that there was in any case nothing to be done till the morn. My counsel finally prevailed, somewhat to my surprise; but not till he had consumed the best part of a quart of his own fiery liquor, by which time of course he was no longer in a condition to go anywhere. I tumbled him into a makeshift bed, and sought my own rest.

Again to my surprise, I slept with relative soundness. I woke at first light; but His Lordship was ahead of me. The cottage was empty; I brewed myself a little tea, then walked up to the head of the glen. I was uncertain quite what I should find; my worst fears, however, were unfounded. The roof of the Great Hall was mostly gone, the tall grid end gaped to the sky; but the rest of the house was unharmed, its stone mullions unscarred, its turrets and chimney pots intact. The grounds were extensively littered with chunks of debris; in their midst the great veteran Rolls stood gleaming and unscathed.

Willie was hopping about among the rubble. He waved cheerfully when he saw me. 'We'll soon hae this tae rights, Jamie lad,' he cried. 'It's nae saw bad at a'. A tarpaulin'll keep oot the wairst o' the wet; mon, we'll rebuild in *style* . . .'

'Rebuild?' said I, stepping back apace.

'Ye heard me well enow,' said he, stroking the bonnet of the Phantom with affection. 'We'll hae this bonny lassie inside too, on a special plinth; so a' the audiences wull see for theirsel' what used tae be. An' what may one day become again . . .'

'Audiences?' cried I. 'But sir, what ye said; aboot the *singin'* . . .'

'I spake nae word o' singin',' said he impatiently. 'But a've had teem f'r *reflection*. Mon, ha' ye e'er considered the wonder o' the *dance*?' He clasped his hands, gazed up at the sky. 'Och, the *line* o' a great ballerina; t'is poetry, Jamie, poetry o' the purest an' most sairtain *keend*. This place wull be famous, mon; its glory will *redoond*, throughout the *wairld* . . .'

'Sir—' I said again.

'We'll start wi' the big *chess combat*,' cried His Lordship happily.

'It shall be the verra first o' all. Can ye no see it, mon? The lines o' wee girl soldiers wi' their wee, wee capes, marchin' on their toes? Then a' the rest. But nane o' y'r modern rubbish, Jamie, nane o' that. Crawlin' aboot on y're lang banes, that's nae the *dance* . . .'

I left him, quietly, and walked back. I sat on my garden wall, filled a pipe and lit it. I smoked it down slowly, enjoying the still, early peace; a peace that, in the nature of things, bade fair to be shattered moderately soon. I tapped the bowl out, and walked toward the cottage; but by the time I reached it the telephone from the big house was already ringing. I shook my head, and stepped inside to answer it. It seemed we were in for a very busy year . . .